THE TONGUE TRADE

MICHAEL J. MARTINECK

EDGE SCIENCE FICTION AND FANTASY PUBLISHING
An Imprint of HADES PUBLICATIONS, INC.
CALGARY

The Tongue Trade

Copyright © 2024 by Michael J Martineck

EDGE SCIENCE FICTION AND FANTASY PUBLISHING
An Imprint of HADES PUBLICATIONS, INC.
P.O. Box 1414, Calgary, Alberta, T2P 2L6, Canada

The EDGE Team:
Producer: Brian Hades
Edited by: Kathryn Shalley
Cover Design: David Willicome
Cover Art: David Willicome
Book Design: Mark Steele

ISBN: 978-1-77053-240-3

EDGE Science Fiction and Fantasy Publishing and Hades Publications, Inc. acknowledges the ongoing support of the Alberta Foundation for the Arts and the Canada Council for the Arts for our publishing programme.

Canada Council Conseil des arts
for the Arts du Canada

FIRST EDITION
(20240615)
Printed in USA
www.edgewebsite.com

Publisher's Note:

Thank you for purchasing this book. It began as an idea, was shaped by the creativity of its talented author, and was subsequently molded into the book you have before you by a team of editors and designers.

Like all EDGE books, this book is the result of the creative talents of a dedicated team of individuals who all believe that books (whether in print or pixels) have the magical ability to take you on an adventure to new and wondrous places powered by the author's imagination.

As EDGE's publisher, I hope that you enjoy this book. It is a part of our ongoing quest to discover talented authors and to make their creative writing available to you.

We also hope that you will share your discovery and enjoyment of this novel on social media through Facebook, Twitter, Goodreads, Pinterest, etc., and by posting your opinions and/or reviews on Amazon and other review sites and blogs. By doing so, others will be able to share your discovery and passion for this book.

Brian Hades, publisher

Dedication

For Sarah, Nina, and Max. My favorite words.

Acknowledgements

If you like this novel at all, it is largely due to the tribunal:
Katheryn Shalley, who made the book brighter.
Jenn Cornish, who made it smarter.
Tom Fitzgerald, who edited like only an old friend can.
And special thanks to Brian Hades and the whole EDGE team, who never seem to shy from putting an ovular novel on orthogonal shelves.

Chapter 1

From "Tales without Interpreters"
A doctor, considering a run for public office, commissioned
a political pollster to test the waters. After a few weeks, the
pollster reported back saying, "the results are negative."
The doctor beamed and pressed ahead with his campaign,
leading to a humiliating, expensive, and for him, quite
surprising loss.

I heard two shots from inside the restaurant, though I didn't
know that's what they were at the time. The city is so full of
noise. Upon exiting, I saw the body, sack-like on the sidewalk. Blood oozed from a fresh hole in a man's forehead.
The blood did not spurt or pour. Without a pumping heart
it had no hurry. Nor was it red, like in the movies. At night,
outside, rolling over an ash gray curb, into a gutter, blood
runs black. You don't get that from a dictionary.

My word. I like the phrase, even though I'd never used
it, which is odd, given its broad utility. You can huff it,
draping your wrist over your forehead, feigning a faint. You
can shout it at some new member of your club claiming he
can round the world in eighty days. You can whisper it as
a promise, puffing hope into a heart, which I have done, in
different terms. I took an oath, but I was young. The words
had been mist, ignorable until one night they condensed
around naiveté, good intentions, and a gun.

"Meat crash," the guy next to me said to his companion.

"End user. Let's send." She seemed upset.

My date — oh man, I had a date. A woman. Marin
latched on to me and released a little "oh" from her mouth.
We turned our heads away. Mounted next to restaurant door,

the word 'Rigoletto's' faced us, each letter a half-meter high beaming a steady scarlet. Not blinking, not flickering, just being big and bright, the word had witnessed the shooting, seen the how, what, maybe even the why. Being only one word, it could never tell.

Marin and I slowly turned back toward the mess. The red light from the sign on her fair face made her look embarrassed for wanting to see the body again.

Pieces of skull and blood-matted hair and fleshy stuff mixed messages with the manicotti and Lambrusco in my stomach. Marin also looked like she should've stuck with a large salad. Our bodies knew better than us. We should've listened to them and left.

The air hung humid, normal for Beau Fleuve in August, as normal as the lack of breeze and stars. Bugs collected around the streetlights and the dead man. I've been told city cops hate hot, sticky nights. The populace gets edgy, and the cops get more work to do. Interpreters too.

People gathered. The door man from Rigoletto's, Tony, held them back from the body. An older woman said, "Call a doctor." I mumbled, "If it's not for you, don't bother." This guy needed a doctor like another hole in his head. People filed out of the restaurant, stopping to see why everyone else had stopped. They all looked, inhaled audibly, and began whispering to the nearest person. Marin and I were unable to walk away.

A motorcycle cop arrived. They're always quick. They just wait for crimes like this, a license to zig and zag through traffic like demons chasing the pure. A rule has been broken, let's break some more rules. This cop swung himself off his bike, then started pushing people farther away from the body. His voxbox blared, "Get back," in several common languages. His white helmet and silvery badge glowed soft pink from the restaurant signage. Because he seemed to want it so much, we allowed him to take control.

The ambulance arrived next. Sirens blaring, lights glaring, it hopped over bumps and curves, and I've got to believe a few people, to get to the scene. The paramedics raced out with toolboxes and coolers and machines with hoses and gauges. They must do it out of habit because one look at the blood on the pavement should have told them what they really needed was a mop.

A camera dropped in from overhead, the mini-blimp kind that made no noise. I wouldn't have noticed if it hadn't broken the pattern of light. It looped the area above the body twice then rested on the khaki epaulet of a narrow shoulder. An oversized safari shirt with too many pockets to be useful. How could anyone remember which of the twelve held your quinine? Which had the compass? Matching shorts rolled up to show off remarkably fit and hairless legs. B Carlisle, independent reporter. I'd met them once before, at a charity auction. They were dressed oddly then, too. Tuxedo jacket and kilt. They looked at me and winked. What the hell was that? Use your words.

I went to college with students who wanted to post for a living. I even thought about journalistic pursuits myself for a time. A short time. At school I learned that reporters are pot-clangors. Success is measured in volume and views and not much else. I could see myself looking like Quasimodo after a few years banging around Beau Fleuve so I leapt from that tower. I do consume news, but it's like smoking. I started young, to be cool. Now I can't seem to quit.

"Let's revisit the space." Marin held my arm, pulling my ear dizzyingly close to her mouth. The air from between her lips tickled me all the way in. It pained me to decline. Rigoletto's was a time-share restaurant. The slot I'd borrowed — the second Tuesday of the month at eight o'clock— had passed. As I opened my mouth to suggest a more intimate place for a nightcap, a voice barreled over the drone of the street. "Is there an interpreter present?"

Looking for the source of the question I found more police had arrived. They stood around the deceased. What looked to be the officer in charge — plain clothes, older than the rest — searched the crowd for someone like me.

Marin, still clutching me, ran her thumb back and forth across my upper arm. Blue eyes outshining the ambulance lights, shimmering blonde hair rolling over bare shoulders, lips so ripe ... I remembered my oath. I promise to facilitate free and truthful communication without bias, malice or misfeasance. Words. What is a person without their words?

"Marin, must reschedule," I said "Emergency."

She nodded. I didn't know her well enough to read her face. She worked in politics, making it that much harder. She might have been able to keep that look as I coughed up a mouse. She faded backwards into the crowd.

"Officer." I moved forward, holding my hand up like I'd won a door prize. "Officer. Licensed Private Interpreter Kirst, William out of Burgess and Huxley." I wanted him to know I worked for a respectable interpreting firm and wasn't some ambulance chaser. I had a general license and was cleared for legal work.

"Great." The plain-clothed cop held out his hand. "Bremburg." He was tall and probably in great shape about ten years ago, before the Monday night volleyball games followed by beer and wings settled into just the latter. He was dressed in a dark blue sportscoat and light gray pants. The secretly stretchy kind. Ready for action. He had a firm handshake. I chose to like him.

"Report, officer?" I asked.

"Detective."

"Apologies."

"Interview's 'terped up." Bremburg flicked his hand leftward. My eyes followed the direction. "See if you can make a deal."

The police wanted to interview someone who wouldn't speak without an interpreter, so they wanted me to contract with the witness. Bremburg pointed at a man who stood facing the body, with his head turned as far away from it as he could manage. The guy was tall enough to see over the crowd. In his midfifties, retaining most of his thick, black hair, he had a decent tan. I imagined a well-manicured spouse, a living room that nobody ever sat in, and a very large boat he knew very little about. His banker-striped suit appeared to have been tailored five minutes ago specifically to show off his build. He'd been born with a bank vault chest and paid an ex-Olympic athlete to help him keep it filled.

I walked over to him, introduced myself and held out my hand. He didn't take it. I chose not to like him. I should have left, but if I didn't work for people I didn't like, I'd miss my next car payment. And all that followed. I told myself this guy was no worse than any other ass that took a seat in my office.

"Your preferred dialect?" I asked. Anyone looking at him would figure he spoke a business argot, but I'm a professional. Assuming makes a businessman out of you and me.

"I'm all business," the man replied.

"The police would like a meeting," I said in the same argot.

"You're an interpreter?" He panned the crowd as he spoke.

"Do you want to hire me?"

He looked all over, really hard, at everyone but me. I stood there watching, feeling inadequate and miffed. Self-image is not my strong suit. Thin, twenty-nine, I was not this man's cup of anything, but I wasn't wearing a tinfoil hat and spouting off about the end days either.

"I am your best and final offer tonight," I said after another two minutes of not being acknowledged.

He turned his eyes on me and blinked slowly. "I need you under contract, with full privileges and duties."

"Oral contracts can be binding. With," and I stressed the next word, "remuneration." I wasn't sure if this was true, but I liked saying it to him anyway.

He closed his eyes and slipped his hand into suitcoat. He took out a pen, pinching it from the top like a herring for a trained seal. He extended it to me. "You're hired."

"To?"

"Mr. Arthur Loam."

I took the pen. My hand drooped from the weight. Gleaming black and gold, with a white splotch on top. A Montblanc. Vintage. I'm not an aficionado, but I knew it would cover several hours of service.

"I'll accept the contract."

"Bull."

He chose to speak Business, with a legalese structure. No Marketing bombast. No Engineering or Medical reference so far. Zero phatic speech, so this guy kept his social channels open by power of his presence. An alpha asshole.

I waved to Bremburg, who walked over without haste. I think he studied Loam as he approached. He stopped with a meter between them and locked his eyes onto Loam's.

Bremburg asked, "Did you witness the homicide?"

I turned to Loam. "Were you on hand for the discharge?"

"Yes." He strayed from Bremburg's eyes, still waiting for someone to come out of the crowd. "This man, the dead man, and I moved on from the restaurant. An unforecasted man with a gun appeared and laid claim to our personal assets. The man to my right declined the offer. The unforecasted man discharged him. I made a run at his assets. In a hostile takeover I rested control and took charge. I leveraged the gun without profit. The man moved on with due haste."

I turned to Bremburg, "Victim exits establishment at the same time as Loam, Arthur. Perp accosts, with firearm. The victim struggles and is shot. Loam provides back up, lifts the perp's firearm, and discharges it without a hit. The perp escapes, presumably on foot."

"Yeah. We found the gun where Loam dropped it." Bremburg looked Loam over. He seemed to have the body, and more importantly, the will, to back up the story.

Loam didn't look happy with me. I knew the questions he had tumbling in his head. The translation sounded fallacious, incomplete to the businessman's ear, and I let it. Sometimes an interpreter needs to assure his client that everything's fine. This wasn't one of those times.

"You know the vic?" Bremburg asked.

"Are you associated with the ex?" I relayed.

"I am unaware of any associations," Loam returned.

"Negative," I said.

"Can you finger any other witnesses?" Bremburg asked.

"Were any other parties on hand at the event?" I asked Loam.

"No." He went back to scanning the crowd.

I didn't need to translate that.

Bremburg went on asking for a description of the shooter, how many times had Loam fired the gun — once — and then asked if they could swab the skin on his dominant hand. That stopped everything. Loam declared the meeting over until his lawyer was in attendance. Bremburg weighed things in his mind. He could press the issue, or he could interview some of the other folks on his list. Bremburg walked towards Tony the doorman, which was fine with me. Hot, sick of standing on concrete, and having lost my date, the time had come to put this night to bed.

I really admire people who can see a defining moment with clarity. They know when to take their shot or make their pass. They respond deftly to a blown engine and bring their blimp in for a single-point landing. I can see all the warning signs like tower lights, straight and bright, but not out in front of me where they would have been useful. I only get them in hindsight. We admire most the traits we don't possess.

A bent, silvery man approached us; Loam reached out and clenched the man's shoulder like a walking-stick. "My attorney, Able Scuttle," Loam said.

"You on retainer?" Scuttle threw the words at me.

I showed him the Montblanc.

He flexed his nose. "Give me the brief," he said to Loam.

I turned to Loam as well. "Legal needs an executive summary of tonight's events."

Loam moved the three of us into a huddle. He dropped his head to angle his voice at the pavement.

"I just discharged Paul Dombrowski. Permanently."

It is highly unprofessional for interpreters to react to something said by a client. It's downright embarrassing when a lawyer's got to push your mouth closed.

We broke from our huddle. Scuttle tweaked the bridge of his nose. I stretched my neck and caught sight of the big, glowing Rigoletto's sign and nodded. We were on the same page, that word and I.

I knew who the killer was and just like that one stupid word, I couldn't tell a soul.

Chapter 2

From "Hoe of Babylon"
A new study by the Blair Foundation advances the argument that cyber argot should be considered for language status.
If cyber syntax [Then]
[go to]
If cyber grammar[Then]
[go to]
If cyber communicates non-cyber information [Then]
[go to]
If cyber does not communicate to non-cyber [Then]
Cyber is a language. Whether anyone can use it for a successful pick-up line is unresolved.

The red and blue flashes pulsed on the glass of the buildings across the street. My Saab was in a lot. I leaned back against a fender wishing I bought a more orthogonal car. This half-popped bubble forced me to brace myself, digging in my heels to keep from sliding off. It was a core workout when I wanted a feather bed. I wasn't headed to one because I knew nothing would help relax me just yet.

I slipped my hand in my right pants pocket, pulled out my silver cigarette of a phone, fanned out the screen, and told it to show me the oath I took the day I was granted an interpreter's license.

Of sound mind and sober condition, I vow to propagate free and truthful communication without bias, malice, or misfeasance, and to confine communication therein without exception.

We took an entire class on that last part. It is so boring a subject that one is apt to forget its parts and functions. The school fights against boredom with repetition. Fifteen weeks of what-ifs and adjoining case law. It all made the answer to my dilemma simple: There was no dilemma. Interpreters are not psychologist or lawyers or priests. We do not offer a service; we are channels to a service. The string between two cans. As such, we do not analyze anything we transmit. Theoretically, we should not know if anything we convey is criminal. We are supposed to gab and forget. Many — most — clients would be happy to wipe our memories clean after a session. When that device debuts, I will take my savings and purchase a pretzel cart. I don't know when that day might come because interpreters are not mediums. There are no interpreter carve-outs in the law for preventing the furtherance or perpetration of crime because we cannot see the future. Given our inability to analyze and our lack of memory, we are less equipped to forecast than a phone. We don't ask phones to sus out crimes. We can't ask interpreters, either.

Or so our guild's lawyers argued. And won. And wrote laws absolving us from ever having to say to a cop, "That guy's a freaking murderer." We are catalysts, not causes. *Facilifurniture* the slur goes. Fixtures in a room. It has to be that way. People must feel they can speak freely or they won't speak at all. The wheels will come off society and everything will skid to a bloody mess.

Shooting someone in the head is, in fact, an even faster way to get to a bloody mess. Still, society seems to need a certain amount of systemic risk. See: Guns, booze, elections.

In the course of becoming an interpreter you are taught to be an empty vessel, an instrument, a horn of sorts. Clients blow in one end, and you expunge out your other, shaping the sound, but never altering the strength or tone or intent. I've never figured out which of my ends did what. I managed to graduate with a degree in English Sublingua just the same. I secured a decent job at a decent firm and forgot about all those contrived, made-up, fake scenarios from Ethics in Translation 101.

Until I couldn't, because I'd stumbled into a real one. That man again, with the blood and brain tissue....

Alright, fine, I told myself. Fully embrace what you can't avoid. Let's think. Loam's lawyer offered no hint of surprise. The flow of the conversation seemed, to me, more of a confirmation than an announcement. As if Loam had reported something expected, rather than springing a surprise. It was the way he'd said, "Paul Dombrowski." He offered no modifying phrase. He didn't say, "a man named Paul Dombrowski," or, "some guy named Paul Dombrowski." Nope. Loam told Scuttle he'd killed Dombrowski as he might discuss fourth quarter earnings.

Put your horn back in its case, William. That is what a good little interpreter would do.

I picked up my head and looked around. Most of the action had subsided. The restaurant had closed, and the crowds had faded into the steam of the night.

Loam had looked around, too, I recalled. It had taken him a long time to commit to the conversation. Distraction is normal in my line of work. Most people understand just half of what's going on anytime I'm present, otherwise I wouldn't be present. Loam, however, did not suffer from uninterest. He searched for something or someone.

All of which was none of my business. What did Loam say? *I'm all business.* Making him my opposite. And opposites repel, right? I never took any Physics. I hoped to God it wasn't another force.

"Hey."

To my right. B Carlisle approached in a steady, slightly hippy walk that made no noise. Black sneakers. Olive socks.

"Saturn Club," I said. "A fundraiser."

"For World Spine Outreach," they replied. "I'm flattered you remember."

"You make an impression."

"What? No adjective?" They stopped and crossed their arms. The stiffness of the khaki shirt made it rise and tent.

"I didn't have one handy."

"I thought maybe you were practicing to be a reporter." They started a smile.

I huffed. "You'll get no competition from me."

"I didn't realize that might be insulting." Smile gone.

"I've got nothing against your profession," I replied. "I just don't think I could do it, is all."

"What part?"

"I don't know. Haven't given it much thought?"

"You're not terrible at the talking part."

"Maybe it's the prying part. Isn't that where we're headed?"

"How did it go over there?" They head-bobbed in the direction of the restaurant.

"Couldn't say," I said.

"You didn't see anything before you went on the job?"

"I came out after it was all over."

"How long after?"

"You a cop?"

"Hardly." It was Carlisle's turn to huff. An imitation of mine. A good one, but I didn't like it. "I make a living off the truth."

"You make a living off conflict. No offense."

"It's fair," they said. "You've got to chip off the barnacles to see the treasure."

"Cops don't do that?"

"You watch."

"No, you watch," I said. "I'll listen."

"I'll do more than watch." They moved the more misbehaving waves of hair back behind their ears. "I'll participate."

"I'll—"

"Nope." They shook their head so slightly. "You can't, can you? You're all twisted up over here, alone in a parking lot. You can't even go home you're so lost in the moment. I get it. I've seen it before. Sometimes it leads to impotence. But, once in a while, every so often, it leads to impetus. If it's ever the later, you know where to find me."

They turned and walked away. That walk that made their hips seesaw, pumping the butt cheeks up and down. Up and down. Massaging the asshole between them. The core of this person, right? The reporter's essence?

Eh. I interlocked my fingers and made a head hammock with my hands. I leaned my skull back into it, eyes up to the skyline. This parking lot sat in the shallows of the city, outside downtown's taller, prouder structures. From my semi-reclined position, I could see the glass and steel towers, stone steeples and marble struts. Mismatched heights, clashing styles — the structures' ages spanned three centuries — and a panoply of purpose. The big buildings looked superior to the others. And they knew it. And they lorded over the two-story shops and doubles and cafes like they were better than all the other huddled, hard-working properties.

A Zeppelin lumbered into view, its gray bulk bathing in the rising city lights, red nose blinking in slow-dance rhythm. Easing in from off the lake, heading for a dock at the Statler Building's needle. From where I leaned, it looked to be as big as the building it would use to park. Fat, calm, so quiet it seemed unreal. Occasionally humans get it right. After almost two hundred years of banishment, lighter-than-air craft roam the skies again. My father took my older — and only — sister and I to see the first of the new breed dock in Beau Fleuve. Family legend has it I cried, scared of the whale in the sky. Being two years old at the time, I can't say as I recall, though that feeling, that quantum of fear cowering under the belly of a great looming beast — I can still sense it inside me, at my sapling core.

I sometimes wonder if everyone doesn't feel that way and that's the real, unspoken reason we went without the Zeppelins, dirigibles, and blimps for so long. All those fears about hydrogen? A conspiracy, my sister always claimed. A hoax perpetrated by the airlines and trucking industries in order to keep a tight hold on, well, holds. Maybe it wasn't. Maybe it was our inner inferiorities.

We got over them, regardless. Yay us. Hydrogen gave loft to logic. Again. Flight without burning billions of gallons of fossil fuel, roasting the environment, and killing all the penguins and such. We as a people overcame our fears.

I would, too.

I sat up. Things would be put right. The murder, the murk behind it, the madness in me — I didn't need to shoulder this weight. It would be lifted by the system, as if by a big hydrogen-filled balloon.

The levity untwisted me. So there, B Carlisle. Not impetus or impotence, I choose imp ... imp ... implosive. I'm going to suck in some air and stop.

Chapter 3

From "Tales without Interpreters"
The Congressman said, "They are going to sanction your
company." So the arms manufacturing executive hired
more people, bought more equipment, and got ready for the
government money to start rolling in. After the legislature
voted, all contracts ceased. The executive screamed in
the foulest way about the gap between politicians and the
truth. Three weeks later he filed for bankruptcy.

The secret hung on the back of my head like an unwelcome chimp. It pulled on my subconscious, making me unbalanced. I shaved my teeth, brushed my face, and applied deodorant to my shoulders, the whole time thinking: I'm working for a murderer. I interpreted a confession putting me in league with a criminal. Party to conspiracy. How the Hell was I going to listen to people chatter away about return on investment or causality clauses when that crap chewed my brain? My Wednesday was already going to be a sack of sand — marketing meetings and over-due time logs and no one interesting with whom to lunch. Nothing offered adequate distraction from the heavy, clawing distraction. The secret. *Secret Chimp*, I sang in my head. Great title for a cartoon. In each episode the arboreal critter drops onto an innocent victim and drives them up a tree. Ha.

As I dressed — light blue suit, today, very cheery — I calmed myself with confidence in the police. They would figure out Loam was a murderer without any assistance from me. They always solve their cases. At least in the movies I like.

To further the cheer, I clipped my new Montblanc pen inside my left breast jacket pocket. Its prestige and wealth

would radiate, imbuing me with gravitas. Never mind that
it tugged the pocket down leveraging the jacket open on one
side, wrecking my outfit's symmetry, and interfering with
my actual movements. The pen remained the esteemed,
conspicuous staff of a wordsmith. I found my phone, and
peeked through the window at the weather.

Despite more than sixty-five thousand geo-synchronous
satellites circling the Earth, beaming down information
with speed and consistency, meteorologists never forecasted
accurately in Beau Fleuve. They say rain, it might snow.
They say snow, you might be searching for your bottle of SPF
450. All one can do is open your senses and guess at the next
twenty minutes. I'd spent two class days on meteorology's
argot. That's enough to realize you need forty more. Coriolis,
katabatic, isobar? These don't have a lot of equivalents in
other lingos. One of the many dangers in my business is the
beat of the pause. If it takes too long to translate a word,
interpreters suffer an urge to skip it. We don't like to look
ignorant, and even a voxbox can fail. But from the other end,
if the translation is ultra-accurate, and thus too long — *A
line connecting two points having equal atmospheric pressure
over a set period of time*, instead of *isobar* — the recipient
won't take it in. The communication becomes holey, and we
all end up in parkas on a ninety-seven-degree day.

I asked the car to take me to work and shoot me the
day's headlines. It crossed my mind to check out B Carlisle's
posts. Would they be intriguing? Puzzling? Nope. Stick to
the routine. This was just another Wednesday. I listened
and kind of watched the posts. No Zeppelin explosions.
Nice. Climatologists were already predicting this to be the
hottest year on record, beating last year, which beat the year
before that, in a chain of bestings going back more than a
hundred and thirty years. Nice, with sarcasm. The National
Association of Professional Interlocutors made "..." an
official English language word. A form of ellipsis, it meant
something left out. In other words: nothing. Protests from
interpreters around the country had already begun.

Yeah, I thought. And I'm one of them. You can't
pronounce three dots. Did they expect you to say, "Dot dot

dot"? Like an espresso machine done brewing? Words need to be said or they are pictures, and I didn't go to school to speak in pictures.

I took my news in English. My phone scanned the mornings posts per my preferences and broadcast them through my car. It knew to skew post towards things that might interest an interpreter in my part of the country. Words, cars, restaurant reviews, tragedies that could interfere with my day. I did not, oddly enough, ever tell my phone to scan the mornings posts for mentions of me. So, my orange Saab slid into its designated slot in the office parking area with me blissfully ignorant inside.

The building in which Burgess and Huxley occupied two floors was a ho hum, glass box that frosted inside during the summer, and baked you in the winter. Its most interesting, irritating feature was the odd and even elevators. Some fitness zealot somewhere believed that if half the elevators went to only even numbered floors and the other half only went to odd numbered floors, it would promote exercise. It promoted the use of expletives. I started collecting them soon after I accepted a position with the firm. Within a week I could tell whether strangers had small children at home — they used sweet swear-word fill-ins like *fudge* —, what they did for a living — accountants use *fold* for some reason — or if English was their base language. *Cac* is my favorite foreign cuss so far. I heard it from an Irish diplomat. When I asked what it meant he'd said he would kick me where it came from if I didn't help him find the eighth floor.

"Morning, Will." Kai Farino hovered at the coffee machine. Not quite thirty, not quite six feet tall, with a not quite filled-in dusty blond beard almost everyone told him to put out of its misery. He and his new girlfriend thought it looked rugged. I knew by the time she became 'Kai's old girlfriend', she would understand that the most rugged thing he ever did was lighting Sterno for fondue. Kai had the extraordinary ability to take a suit, costing maybe a month's salary, put it on and appear to have slept in it. Everybody liked him, he was a talented interpreter, and he never asked you for money.

"Someone's evening was ... variegated." He smiled and slurped his coffee.

"What do you mean?"

"The murder, the police, the blonde dollop in the white sheath? Ah, the spice of life."

I had no idea how he could have had these details. I had not seen him, or any mutual associate, at the restaurant.

"How do you know what I did last night? What's it all over the po—"

"You didn't scan the morning posts, did you?"

"No. Yes. I've been ... abstracted."

"You'd better come to my office."

My black mug — that displayed the current temperature of its contents with little red numerals — sat clean in the kitchenet cabinet. I filled it with matching coffee and followed Kai. The bounce in his walk gave me a bad feeling.

With a large grin he rounded his cluttered desk, pivoted his silky monitor, and there I was, in full color, mouth gaping and dumb. Marin clutched my arm. The camera that had swooped through the scene gleaned a cluster of images before I went to work for Loam. The dead guy's legs lay in the foreground, other bystanders lingered in the background. B Carlisle's post had shown atypical taste in not running a shot with more splatter and tissue. The gory pictures must not have turned out too well.

Kai chuckled.

"I don't believe this," I said.

"Hey, it's not a bad picture, really. No sound or motion, though...." True. It could have been worse. Luckily movement would have added little to the story. No fire, no car chase. "That could not have been your date. Beautiful and smart enough to realize she could yank you in front of her if the shooting started again?"

"She's one of Congressman Freeman's aids. After ditching her for a pick-up, I may have to move out of his district."

Kai's eyes swelled to the size of golf balls. He swung his screen around to use them. He spun the screen back again and placed his index finger next to Marin's image.

"You took a side job with her hanging on your arm? Your arm? The arm of William Kirst who hasn't had someone touch him since that Sally girl from downstairs got drunk and played 'I've got your nose' at that retirement party. What possessed you to tell anyone you're a mouthpiece?"

"It was my duty. I took an oath, just like you did. I meant it."

"Like I didn't?"

"I didn't say—"

"Nah, you're right. I figured this was an easy way to meet women. Learn to speak their language, so to speak."

Back in my office, I read the article twice. The first pass smeared things in my mind. The second had a modicum of clarity, though what it made clear was a dirty lie.

Stern and reticent, Arthur Loam reluctantly admitted to bravely thwarting the mugging, saving his own life, and perhaps keeping countless others from following Paul Dombrowski's fate, falling to the concrete, to be fleeced and left for dead. The torment on his face came from the fact that he could not save this other man. If he had been just a moment faster, if he had shunned the lemon panna cotta, maybe ... accomplished, wealthy, magnanimous, now tormented.

I had read B Carlisle's stuff before. This one was off. Too many adjectives. I couldn't shake the feeling it was aimed at me.

Other posts had picked up the story. Some rounded it out. The search for the assailant continued. Tony the doorman got mentioned as a person of interest. The police had not treated him as such last night. Now they murmured about a partner in crime, someone to call out rich targets and make sure the cameras caught nothing. If the police were on the same page as the news, Arthur Loam would get away with murder and an innocent man would get the shaft. All of which had to be put into the back of my mind and sealed off. I couldn't work this way. I had lots of ways I couldn't work. A new one need not apply.

My first meeting would, I hoped, cause me to focus. Some direct marketing people were meeting a prospective client, a woman who ran a parenting-consultation firm. Before I began interpreting for the two parties, I had nothing resembling a care as to what a parenting-consultation firm did. Now I repeated the details like they had been obvious from the start. I learned that these parenting consultants sent a qualified representative into your home for a fortnight. The consultant sat in the corner and watched everything you did. How much quality time you spent with your kid, what entertainment you allowed, how you handled a crisis like the shoving of a shrimp fork into your Bang & Olufsen speakers. They watched it all. Then they issued you a detailed analysis of your parenting skills. The direct marketing people wanted to develop a message salvo that would penetrate every household with a child between two weeks and sixteen years old, in the greater Beau Fleuve area, convincing moms and dads that they needed this service.

Nothing against marketing professionals, but theirs is my least favorite tongue. It's difficult to translate because of all the ambiguity purposely built in. In most cases the marketing people have said nothing and are hoping the interpreter will invent something to tell the client. How do you say to a developmental psychologist that it pops, grabs, or smacks 'em in the face without that psychologist thinking you're not describing a pro wrestling match? Developmental psychology doesn't have the necessary unnecessary words. Most tongues lack commonality with Marketing, no cognates — words that correlate in the argots. Like *killer* and *murderer*. Those are close enough to transfer meaning. As opposed to *murderer* and *Tony*, which had no common meaning.

And already I was backsliding.

I faked my way through the meeting continuously reminding myself not to think about shots to the head and conspiracies, and concentrate on the woman with big, gold earrings tell the woman with big, silver earrings that her firm will "Drive the target through an immersive three-sixty- win-win." Or, as best I could manage, "Their behavior will result in the desired outcome."

Lunch happened at my desk: I ate something I'd exhumed from the automat under the impression that it would be a turkey wrap. It might have been a creamed corn sarcophagus for all I noticed. The large monitor on my desk glowed with research. Cathartic research. Not being able to kill off my thoughts of homicide, I embraced them instead.

Paul Dombrowski, age sixty-four, had owned a small vineyard outside of Lockport, New York, up in the pastoral regions of Niagara County, a place I hadn't visited since my grandfather passed away. Paul enjoyed historical fiction, woodworking, and occasionally volunteered for a charity that raised money for cancer research. Four years a widower from his husband of close to thirty years, Alex Lightwood, the data made him seem nice. No criminal record. No bankruptcies. No outstanding leans. No uncrossed T's or undotted I's.

The computer failed to overlap Paul and Arthur Loam. As far as I could tell, the Venn diagrams of their lives bounced off each other, without a sliver of shared space. Something had to connect them. Paul didn't get shot to death for nothing.

Loam's public profiles were marvels of structure and form. So many words conveying so little information. It took skill to get that seriously empty. The tidbits that did survive: Loam sat on the board of the Beau Fleuve Philharmonic, the Art Gallery, and the Olmsted Park Conservancy — three of the showiest and most important nonprofits in the city. He seemed to own a lot of property, including four office buildings, three major Zeppelin docks, and the apartment building I lived in. Comforting. He also appeared at a lot of Conservative Party fundraisers. Not the kind that helped cure diseases. The only word Loam and Dombrowski had in common was *male*.

One learns after a few years of interpreting that it's not always what's said that's important, sometimes it's what gets left out. Valuable content can nestle in the unsaid. Loam's curriculum vitae shined so bright I could see the swirls from the polishing. I think he had professionals curating his virtual presence. On the computer screen, he came across like Santa's nicer brother. But I had met him and if he got his hand in your stocking, he wouldn't be leaving you a toy.

Research never slakes your thirst for research. I decided to scratch that into the stall wall next time I was indisposed. I could use my Montblanc.

My afternoon offered a sit-down with a retired doctor and his lawyer. My lawyer. Ex, er … lawyer and all. Normally I would have treated the meeting as one might cross a frozen river barefoot. Today, I had worse things on my mind than Isla Vokevitch, esquire.

When I part with a girlfriend, I part for good. None of this Lets-Be-Friends crap. No occasional calls, Christmas cards, or vapid conversation in the drugstore, while you're trying to see if they're buying home-pregnancy tests or jumbo-sized condoms. All my ex-girlfriends really really don't care for me, avoid and ignore me, and all for the same reason: Something I said.

Whenever I say, "Was it something I said?" the answer is always, "Yes, good-bye, call me and I'll put an air-horn to that part of the phone you talk into." With Isla I made it to a seventh date. Being an attorney, she had thick shell. My inevitable slips-of-the-tongue would roll off her back, like rain on a fresh coat of Turtle Wax. At least for a while.

Our romance ended much the way our universe began. She invited me to a party tossed by one of the three hundred legal associations to which she belonged. I didn't mind getting dressed up in my best — handpicked by her — clothes. I didn't mind being introduced as Isla's friend. I didn't mind being told "One martini an hour; I'm keeping track." I minded the room, full of people who never figured out why Judas hanged himself. I mean, he got twenty pieces of silver, right? That bought a nice piece of waterfront back then.

"I'm surprised you don't caucus better with my associates, Will," she'd said.

"They don't all see it that way," I remember replying. "Most don't see me at all. They ask me what kind of law I practice; I confess to interpreting and they redirect their attentions. I feel like I wore jammies to a black-tie."

"You're not underdressed."

"Under-classed for this gallery."

"Civility, please." She gave me a look designed to tell me my usual comments would not be appreciated. All her friends had passed the bar, so putting them back in the gallery could be taken as an insult. Especially if I offered it that way.

"There's a great deal of commonality," Isla continued. "Lawyers possess the same love of language that you do. Language allows us to coadjute. To process. In sum, the law is language."

"The law is a language's bastard son. Lawyers make a living adjoining meanings, claiming tacit meanings, and excluding meanings of words, with disregard for the true definitions. Twist it. Turn it. 'What you really meant to say was black, not white, correct?'"

"All words have multiple meanings. The process of law decides the true meaning for the moment."

"Truth is not pro tempore," I'd said.

"Truth is not found in a word, it is derived from it," she returned.

"Attorneys are not hearty miners, digging for the truth, whistling while they work. They're hucksters, trying to get you to buy their version."

"And what are interpreters?" Isla asked. "Are they consigned to the truth, or do they just orate whatever they hear like human tubes. Parrots for the prosecution?"

"Out of order."

"You're the hostile party."

The song had ended. People had formed a circle around us, like we were the best jitterbuggers in the room. None would have rather seen us dance. Argument is the true lawyer art. Painting, song, verse — all birthed in conflict. Perform for us the pure art, the argument, they all said to themselves.

"I'm calling a recess." I took her hand and we walked from the center of everyone's attention.

She came up close to my ear for the last time ever.

"In omnibus terminus."

When I got home, I had to put a heating pad on that side of my head. The frost penetrated to my medulla oblon-everything. It flared up again as I entered the conference room.

Isla wore her sunny hair to the shoulder on one side and nearly to the scalp on the other. The imbalance said devilish, but under control. She sat with her long legs crossed tightly under her wheat-colored skirt. Her starchy striped blouse puckered and called to me. A willowy landscape. A van Gogh. No, a Vokevitch. She had created this scene with care and talent.

Her client, a man between the ages of ten and ninety, also sat somewhere in the room.

The greetings came and went, and the client got to the point like a person fully aware that he burned the cost of a good shoeshine every second he spent with us. Essentially, the guy wanted data from a private Zeppelin line about usage, patterns and demographics. They declined. He wanted to sue. I had no idea why he wanted the information, other than fulfillment of his destiny as a cranky old guy.

"You have no standing," Isla stated. "I would very much like to pursue the case, as that is how I earn a living, but with no protectable interests you will never make the docket."

"The carrier's lack of response is without complication," I interpreted. "Legal approves of the procedure in general. This is how they bill. But the judge will deny outright."

The doctor looked a little angry, a little confused. "There is systemic harm from the carrier's negligence."

I said, "The client claims indirect injury from mis, mal or nonfeasance as party to a class."

Isla bent forward, rolling her lips into position for a possible, future smile. She exuded pliancy, receptiveness, fun. She looked from her client to me and back, then said. "Dead on arrival."

No need to interpret that bit.

The doctor thanked us, said he understood without conviction, and left. Isla's back went straight, the fun left her face and she collected her stuff.

"Sidebar?" I asked.

"Full docket today." She gave not a glance.

"As pertains to my oath."

This earned me a dart of the eyes.

I asked, "Is interpreter confidentiality like …. you know … how vitamins have a stated expiration clause, but you can still ingest them sine die?"

"Good God, what did you do?"

"Nothing. Yet. I mean, I need consul as regards future activity."

"Settle yourself," Isla said. "I do not want to be party to your premeditation. Understand this: the confidentiality of interpreters is pretty ironclad. Both ways. No authority can force testimony, testimony cannot be put forth willingly. Except in exigent circumstances. Can your statement guarantee to prevent additional, irreparable harm?"

"That is not clear at this time."

"You need to continue executing your end of the contract implicit in every interpretive session in which you participate, actively or inactively. There is reasonable assumption of confidentiality in perpetuity."

"But the consequences...."

"Are commensurate with the transgression. You learned all of this in school."

"You'd be shocked by what escaped me in school."

"Be careful with your license, Will. No one looks favorably on a disbarred interpreter. Violations of trust follow you in perpetuity, too."

We let that hang there in the air. She got up, and walked to the door as if the room were empty.

"Thank you," I said. "I appreciate the advice. You're kind...."

She stopped, but didn't turn. "Kind of what?"

"I ... just...."

"Thanks." She almost looked over her shoulder "No one's ever said I was just. And I do try."

My phone sent a pulse through my thigh before I could correct her, probably for the best. She left as I tapped the device in my pocket.

"Kirst," I said.

"Change," Victoria, my supervisor superior, said.

"I'd like to," I replied. "Maybe a self-help seminar would—"

"Conference Room Chesterton. Ten minutes." Click.

Interpreters tend to dislike last-second substitutions. Most of us prepare, in some manner, for whatever kind of session we're going to work. We may read files on the topics at hand. We may catch up on recent changes to argot or usage in the languages that will be used. Some trades add words daily, with the newest always flashing to the forefront faster than general interpreters can manage. So, Victoria's request irritated me. Having to run to another meeting without a break irritated me more. I entered the conference room and my irritation evaporated. I didn't have room for annoyance and terror at the same time.

Arthur Loam waited for me.

Chapter 4

From "Tales without Interpreters"
The marketing manager asked the man next door what
the mule deer were doing in her English garden. She'd
put a lot of work into the shaped shrubs. He was a farmer
and seemed to know everything so when he said, "They're
browsing," she said, "Fine. As long as they don't buy." She
laughed and went off to work, never to see her topiaries
again.

Ignoring the twitch in my stomach, I continued into Conference Room Chesterton and said hello. Loam met me with a strong handshake. Overly strong, I thought. Like he wanted to take off his shirt and flex but knew it just wasn't done. I noticed Able Scuttle, and forced my face to stay placid as I greeted him with a nod.

Neither man made any kind of sign that they knew me. I wasn't expecting a slap on the back and a "Hey, that was some murder last night, huh?" But these men were too aloof, trying too hard. I told myself to ignore and go forth. They didn't want to talk about last night and I couldn't. Time to function.

Across from us sat David Potts and his attorney. Potts orbited seventy years of age, was gaunt, and seemed harmless. His lawyer, Felber, appeared equally subdued. They both wore suits and ties and trim haircuts, but not the right suits and ties and trim haircuts. They were perhaps very nice people if one could pay attention long enough to find out. I wouldn't know. Loam and Scuttle tugged at my attention, never giving my mind more than a moment away.

I leaned over the table and shook two more hands. The lawyer said, "Honor," Potts said "Pleasure," and I sat down at the head of the table.

"William Kirst of Burgess and Huxley, general interpreter, contracted for this meeting," I said to the businessmen.

"Kirst, William, legist interpreter, lex loci contractus communicatio, Burgess and Huxley," I said to the lawyers.

I liked this room. The walls were an unexciting beige, but the table was real oak, and the chairs were plump and soft. This room meant it would be a high-powered meeting. That part I didn't like. I had no taste for a high-powered Loam.

"One-hundred-year lease contract, Niagara County plot 433-56, all structures therein, rights transfer, ipso facto, vender to vendee, upon verified identify and funds." Scuttle passed his large, yellow legal screen over to Felber, who took in the terms. Potts glanced over at the reader as well, but it was for effect. He couldn't read more than four words of the contract. I kept thinking, one-hundred-year lease? Who did that? Why not just transfer ownership? Was there a practical difference between buying and leasing for a century?

The next thirty minutes ping-ponged environmental studies, zoning restrictions, easements and assurances that the land had not, at one time, been used for the interment of the deceased.

I halted over the last translation. The de-what? In the previous three years I'd facilitated more than fifty real estate transactions. For property deals people really want to get the language right. A clause about one of those properties being a graveyard had never arisen.

"To the best of our knowledge," I said to Loam, "this parcel has never been purposed as a cemetery."

"Burial ground," he returned.

"What?" jumped out of my mouth.

"Not cemetery. Burial ground," he corrected me.

My neck caught fire. I could feel my face fill with hot blood. Never, never had I been corrected by a client. And he wasn't even right. Current business vernacular for a place in which the dead are interred, is *cemetery*.

Loam looked at me, his face heavy. He had no anger or even frustration. He showed a tepid impatience with my not catching up to him. He wanted my little rabbit mind to dart around my inner dictionary, possibly protest, recall some nonsense about the customer being right and him being the customer and—

This guy was an asshole.

Regardless of his assholiness, I had no choice but to turn to Mr. Potts and ask, "Has this parcel ever been purposed as a burial ground."

"No," Potts returned.

I looked at Loam, who had already turned away. He pointed to something on Scuttle's reader.

After another quarter of an hour Felber announced, "Agreed terms satisfied, compensation at parity, in toto."

Loam and Potts looked up at me, waiting for some clue as to what might be transpiring.

"Price met by leasor and leasee," I told them. I made a point of using the most recent argot, not the lessor and lessee Potts and Felber might have preferred.

"Contract report?" Loam asked. Potts nodded his head in agreement. I picked up the reader and buzzed through the contract. All of the usual lease lingo looked back at me. With the additional burial ground proviso. The only structure mentioned was a Zeppelin tower. Reconstruction had finished up last week. Curious. Those things usually sprouted up around all sorts of other things — people, warehouses, manufacturing facilities. Not farmland. I had so many questions and no right asking even one. The contract said what they all said it said. I assumed Loam and Potts didn't want me to translate out loud and simply announced, "Black."

They smiled.

Felber passed over a piece of beautiful linen stationery, a printed version of the contract. The room recorded everything that transpired therein, obviating the need for any kind of paper. I smiled.

Scuttle chuckled at the old fashion touch. Potts grinned, signed it, and passed it to Loam. Loam patted his chest and turned to me. He continued to pat his pocket where his Montblanc had hung the night before.

I drew the pen out of my pocket and handed it to him. His mouth curled on the left. I couldn't tell if he fought a smile or lacked the ability to complete one. Did he chuckle coldly inside, to himself? At me? Interpreters are forced to take all kinds of silly, day-filling college courses designed to milk more tuition out of students. I put any class beginning with the words nonverbal in that category. Loam's smile exemplified why. It gave me a chill. Were I a chef, physicist, or frog who'd never been afforded the opportunity to study *nonverbal* communication, I still would have felt the sensation of cool oil dribbling down my spine.

Loam signed the contract and gave me back the pen.

"It's a fine parcel, Mr. Loam. Happy returns." Potts stood and held his hand across the table. I gathered he was pleased with the money this lease brought.

"Bull." Loam pumped his hand once. The attorneys stood and shook hands and everyone but Loam smiled. In a few minutes they were gone, the deal done. I sat back down at the head of the table and plopped my face into my hands.

Loam had corrected me.

As the anger and humiliation dissipated, I trembled. Not visibly. Not with quakes or random flicks you see in interpreters that have finally blown their Broca's. No, my body did not know what to do with its current cocktail of endorphins.

It's not that I hadn't been corrected before. My teachers had called out errors like auctioneers calling out bids at estate sales. It is, after all, how we learn. But never in my life had I been more offended by a suggested word choice. Never in my life had I been more offended by anything at all, ever.

You've got to punch through this, I said to myself.

Or not, I argued back.

I worked back through the session, checking my notes and contemplating the little things that troubled me.

Loam had to have a scant knowledge of Juris or he would have asked more questions and made fewer comments. I heard him speak broken Security the previous night and fluent Business today. He understood three languages and still paid for an interpreter. This was not unusual. When you're pushing millions of dollars across the table, you want to be very sure you and the guy on the other side have a mutual understanding.

My read of the contract left me vexed. Loam just leased a small plot of land, and a shiny new Zeppelin tower, in the middle of nowhere. An ellipse of land. The heart of Niagara County hosted cow pastures and not much else. Why would Loam take a position now?

Burial ground. Who used that term outside of horror movies.

As with most children, I spent hundreds of thousands of hours immersed in various forms of speculative entertainment. By the time I was ten, I had viewed the fictitious deaths of over six hundred thousand people. Car crashes, rocket explosions, mob shoot outs, famished aliens, people squashed under the toes of gargantuan lizards, and regular Joes offed because they knew too much. This type of upbringing prepares you for a life of lurking mysteries. Some people outgrow the idea of hidden stories. Some do not. Some, maybe one person in particular, no longer knew which category was his.

Loam had most certainly requested me for the meeting, even though it had nothing to do with the previous night's ruckus. And yet, I had to ask what he was doing in the farms east of Niagara Falls. Today and last night seemed connected by some kind of disconnect.

There is an easy, natural, logical cure for a disconnection. I doubled tapped the control pad on the table to ensure the room would stop paying me any attention. I slipped out my phone and held it between my gesturing finger and that third one that doesn't do too much.

I said, "Detective Bremburg, Beau Fleuve Police Department."

"William Kirst?" the voice on the other end asked.

"That's me."

"This is Bremburg. What can I do for you?"

"I need a face-to-face."

"What's this about?"

"There's the catch," I said. "If I informed by phone, I wouldn't need to face."

"How soon?"

"Forthwith."

"Roger that."

I told him I'd be right over. I had no idea what else I'd tell him. Not much of anything, really. I knew that. Even as I requested the meeting, I knew it was all a front. A form of lie. I wanted to know more without reciprocating. I wanted to feel better without taking my medicine.

I left the room and ran full into Victoria, catching her around the waist so we both remained upright. We twirled and parted. I almost bowed, like we'd been doing a very short Virginia Reel, but stopped myself, briefly relishing the surprised look on her face. The first one I'd ever seen. Victoria, in her short black hair, cut in the style of preoccupied porcupine. Twelve years my senior, she always made me feel the way Siamese cats do when you enter their homes. They stare at you, listen to you, maybe even brush up against you, but they never let you forget that you're in their house, and you'll be watched the entire time that you are for reasons you'll never discern. Thin, poised, she had no problem attracting partners whom she deemed intellectual peers — even if they never would be. She purred in a voice that made me feel like a toddler in trouble.

"My what a hurry."

"Sorry, I have an emergency of sorts."

"I thought the rest of your day was clear." Her tone made it clear that she had made my day clear. The purpose of not being booked for meetings did not outrun my imagination. A professional procrastinator must always keep in mind what must be done, so that he knows what to put off.

"I had hoped that you would be able to complete your time-tracking this afternoon, William." Some would have found her smile sexy. My throat swelled.

"My hopes concur, Victoria." One time a new employee called her Vicki. He was assigned to interpret for chemical engineers eight hours a day, five days a week, until he quit the firm and bought a hotdog cart. "Unfortunately, I have some police business. Did you catch anything about a shooting last night on Elmwood?"

"No."

"I became attached to the homicide investigation. I'm required to make a statement to the police today."

"Can we bill for it?"

"I don't know." I'd already collected my Montblanc. "I guess it's for an existing client, but I agreed to...." Time to evade. "It was kind of a conscription. Pro bono police work, more than likely."

"That should be tracked," Victoria said. "Why can't everything be handled from here? We have certified recording equipment."

"You know the police. They like to do things in person."

"How was your session with Mr. Loam?"

"Adequate," I replied.

"He stopped just short of demanding your assignment."

"Are you surprised one of your protégés has developed a devout clientele?"

"No, William." She gave a small, disapproving smirk. "That would not be what surprised me."

I turned sideways and sidled by. She shook her head. I scooted down the corridor, through the lobby, to the sealed elevator doors. They mercifully parted and I rushed inside, this time slamming into Kai.

"Hey, what's the rush? Late for a nap?"

"I've got to get over to the police station."

"It's not goin' anywhere, Will. Relax."

"I hate being late." The doors closed. I pushed *L*.

"This murder business has you twitchy. You should go out tonight."

I watched the greenish digits on the wall count down, odd numbers only. *Eleven —nine — seven—* "I'll call you later, Kai." *Five — three — L*.

Lobby doors flew open as I charged them. Going outside felt like entering an oven. The humidity hit probably 120 percent. There wasn't any direct sunlight. Just bright haze. Sweat percolated through my pores.

I got into my furnace of a car and looked around to see if any of the black stereo knobs and map switches and one-inch, square, plastic, removable sections — whose only purpose was to remind me that I didn't get every conceivable option installed when I bought the car — had melted into sticky puddles. As I did so, I caught a glance at myself in the vanity mirror. The humidity, perspiration, and running around made my hair frizz out. It cranked up my aggravation.

"Your heart rate is one hundred and fifty-one beats per minute." The car announced. "Is there an issue of which I should be made aware?"

"Copasetic, car." I used my safe word, so it didn't call the police. Like I needed more police. "We're copasetic."

Chapter 5

From "Tales without Interpreters"

A journalist needs to get a post up. She dictates into her computer, even as a technician works to repair her workstation. She sits back to read what she's written and fiddles idly with a nearby wire. "Don't touch that lead," the technician says. Believing the tech had been reading over her shoulder, the journalist thanks him for the compliment, pinches the wire, and gets zapped out of her chair.

The gentleman sitting next to me was in his midthirties, wearing the top half of a tuxedo, costly cross-training shoes, and a handcuff clinked to the arm of his chair. Pants would have been a nice touch, I thought, but they're not for everyone. As with languages, most occupations have their own uniforms too. Engineers need short sleeve shirts with breast pockets for their monocles, UV repairmen need pants that hang low to show off the top part of their buttocks when they bend over to look inside your broken appliance — it distracts you when they start figuring out how much they can take you for — firemen need really big gloves. It had never occurred to me that sex workers would have similar stipulations about wardrobe, with no mandate on trousers.

He smelled great. I wanted to ask him what he was wearing but figured it was probably a trade secret, like magicians and how they knew you'd pick the Queen of Hearts. I also wanted to ask him if the humidity and my nervousness had altered my smell for the worse but figured he might charge for getting that close.

"Eyes on, John. Thirty to buff, fifty to gum," he said with a smile.

"No thank you." I tried to be polite.

"Reds all neg, John. Got the charts. Nobody'll eye."

"No. Really. But thank you." I started looking over the room again. Cops buzzed around, chortling, chugging what I presumed was coffee, and charging suspects. No one paid me or my rent-a-friend any mind. He had more than likely been right when he said what? Nobody'll eye? Nobody would notice any activity between us. Street lingo. Loved it. Learned it. Saved it.

The level of everyone else's activity did not go unnoticed. This felt like a hardware store on the eve of a big blow, as the pilots would say. I had not considered how much trouble hit my hometown. I wondered, for a second, how many mysteries actually got solved.

The door to Bremburg's office opened. The detective looked right at me. "Mr. Kirst."

"Thanks." I got up and made my way into his cubby.

"Maybe later," the guy behind me said. I did not look back.

The walls of Bremburg's office rose higher than the others around the precinct room, enclosing what seemed to be a small flee market. He had three out-of-date monitors set up on his long, plastic desk. The pale, rubbery wires growing from their backs coiled over, across, and through everything else. He went around to sit on his side of the desk and offered me one of two unmatched chairs on the visitor's side. Looking over the mess, past Bremburg, and out the window, I saw a shimmering, azure, tree-lined pond. The sun danced across the water, nurturing your eyes, reminding you that there are still nice places in the world. Places to catch electronically and haul home.

"Should be a trout on the wall," I said as I sat down.

"Home. You a fisher, Kirst?" His face brightened a bit.

"Rookie. Used to partner with my grandfather. Never ranked, though. Talked too much. He said I scared the fish."

Bremburg snickered. "What's the motivation for this face-to-face?"

"I remembered something from last night," I lied. "From before I signed on," I lied some more. "I observed Loam and the vic in conversation prior to their exit."

Bremburg leaned way back in his chair and closed his eyes. I thought he started a nap. Then he opened his eyes back up like his lids weighed thirty pounds each. "What? Like a run-in outside the men's room?"

"Yeah," I replied.

"You seem friendly, Mr. Kirst. You never greet an unknown outside a men's room? Just to be polite?"

"It seemed … I don't know … like more."

"You want to characterize this as a relationship?"

"I couldn't say."

"Seems like you're attempting to say something."

"I'm completing my report."

"Thanks for coming down." He leaned forward and poked his nearest monitor. Without looking up, he asked, "you know Tony Perissi, AKA Tony the doorman?"

"No history," I answered. "No priors with the establishment."

"You couldn't say if Tony was capable of conspiracy to commit homicide?"

That was an odd question. So odd, I didn't think it was the question at all.

"Like you said, I couldn't say."

"You say 'couldn't say' a lot for a mouthpiece."

"Occupational hazard."

"You think maybe we're following the wrong lead?"

"A…." My brain needed time.

While its study is not my passion, 90 percent of all communication is nonverbal. Interpreters spend most of their time on the other 10 percent. Most, not all. I don't savor the mush of the unworded world. It is more divination than derivation. Still, nonverbal information frequently informs oration. It can help you decide between hyperbole and fact, the sarcastic and the sincere, the flippant and the dumb. It offers clues and I could see by this police detective's gaze that while I'd spent the good part of a decade on the smaller portion of interpersonal communication, he had been studying the bulk. He watched all of me, hands, nose, eyes. He could probably smell the confusion on me.

"Is Tony hard up, Mr. Kirst? Financially?" Bremburg's eyes pinned me. "You think he could look the other way while some skell made a snatch?"

Skell? Crap, they thought all wrong. "I'm a good citizen," I replied. "Truth. Justice. Cherry pie and gingham tablecloths, you know? But I don't know."

He leaned forward on the desk and folded his arms over each other. I couldn't tell what he was thinking. I don't know what I looked like, but stress marks must have shown. He thought I was an origami chump, folding under the first hard look from authority.

"You're Loam's mouthpiece," he said.

"One timer."

"He upped with your firm two years ago."

"No priors with him."

"So, it's a coincidence, you two being at the scene."

"Yes."

"Maybe I should like the tooth fairy for this, huh? You thinking I believe in the tooth fairy and coincidences and maybe unicorns too?"

Damn. I don't know what I had been expecting, but it wasn't this.

Bremburg sat back, locking his hands behind his head. "I got an attempted robbery at a scene that hasn't seen one in five years. I got a surveillance camera aimed to the north, instead of south, and a doorman claiming to be investigating a missing umbrella when he should have been a witness. Then you, Mr. Kirst ... You're a word guy, right? You got a word for a four-way coincidence?"

It appeared to be my time to leave.

My car tried to take me back to my apartment, but the traffic remained inert. Rush hour, on a sticky evening, is the second ring of Hell. Many-colored blobs, evenly spaced, idling in wait for a chink in the endless chain of rubber, plastic, and safety glass strung out on the Thruway, ever, for eternity....

I sat in line on the entrance ramp, wondering if there might be a small animal close by that I could sacrifice and offer up to the traffic gods in hopes they'd part the sea of cars. I'd never tried ritual myself, but I've seen the squished remnants of others having done it, so there must be something to it. I would rather have offed a rodent than sat there with my thoughts. Churning, tumbling, useless thoughts. That poor man's dead body, Loam in the conference room, the police tying me into the troubles.

Bremburg had been on a fishing trip. I'd taken him to the ol' fishing hole then almost became the catch of the day. He didn't believe Tony and the fictitious gunman conspired to mug Dombrowski and Loam. He trolled for anything — a bounce of my eyebrows, a long look up and to the right, a nostril twitch — anything that could bring his hunches and his evidence closer together.

Enough. "Car." I woke my Saab's attention. "News, current, English." It already knew the topics I liked.

"A special session of the state legislature will convene Monday. The highly unusual August docket will cover air transit regulations. To hear more, say 'special session.' In related news, an explosion over the Pine Barrens is now a confirmed Zeppelin accident. No word yet on survivors. A logging blimp with a crew of seven caught fire, this is the first inflight flameout for Kovac Transportation, but we've already seen eight major flying conflagrations for this quart—"

"Call Sophia." I listened to the periodic tones of a wanting connection.

"Cavu," my sister's voice cranked through the car speakers.

Oh good, I thought. Ceiling and Visibility Unlimited, and, of course, she's alive to abbreviate that fact. "Copy that," I replied.

"You don't have to punch through every time there's a Zep burning."

"It's a good excuse."

"I'm carting hydrate up the coast today. The weather's perfect."

"Glad to hear it."

"What's your status?"

"Unchanged," I lied. I was pretty much a liar now.

"Okey-dokey, then. I'm gonna keep my eyes high. You good?"

"I am good."

"Over and out."

"Roger dodger."

She laughed a bit as she ended the call. My Saab launched out into a space I wouldn't have guessed fit my trunk. Proving again, the cars know best.

I am good, I repeated in my head. I am good.

I would not stay that way.

A cold shower and colder iced tea. That's all I let myself think about as my Saab rolled into my slot. Being so close to the front door of my building brought a sunny smile to my face. I smiled as the elevator elevated and smiled more as I opened my door.

I stopped smiling. Something smelled wrong.

The climate control system had been set to fill the room with the scent of a fresh, spring rain. With all the moisture stuck in air the last few days, it was mentally relieving to get a whiff of wet grass and pavement. But the air in my apartment brushed over blooming lilacs. It carried the remembrance of sipping lemonade in my grandmother's backyard the first nice day of spring, listening to her stories about the old days and grandpa disagreeing with every third detail. Memories of tag, the tire swing, cousins, mud. It was scent number twelve on the pad and not the one I had selected.

"Mr. Kirst. I'm pleased."

My head spun to face the easy chair in the corner of my living room. Enough light seeped through the drawn sheers to show off a pair of perfectly shaped legs, one neatly resting on the other. My eyes ran from the arresting red shoes, up the sharp shins and waited hesitantly at the knees. It didn't seem like someone I'd kick out of my living room for making it smell nice.

"Andrea Breen. An associate of Mr. Loam." A tenor sax voice. She sat relaxed. Her blue and white seersucker suit looked like a costume. Ruffled hair reminding me of Sunday mornings, eyes still as midnight — nothing else about this woman said *garden party*.

"You already know me, so an introduction would be redundant." I walked into the center of the living room, trying to look cool, but Andrea got better looking with every step. I had no idea how old she was, maybe my age. It didn't matter as much as a couple other things. "May I ask what you're doing in my apartment?"

"Waiting to conference. Is the appointment inconvenient?"

"Not for you, it seems." I wasn't quite sure what dialect she used. The lexicon so far signaled Business with a skirting knowledge of English, but I couldn't be certain.

"Your tongue is lovely. Is it…." That came out wrong. I stopped.

"Mine?" She asked.

"Yes."

The tip of her tongue darted between her lips. "Private property."

"I mean Business. Is your tongue Business?"

"Mostly business."

I took a breath. "You declined to hold a position outside, huh?"

"I don't buy standing."

"Nor should you," I said. "Mind if get a drink?"

"Make it a joint venture."

"Why didn't you help yourself?"

"I like proposals."

"What'll you have?"

"What would you like?"

The thought of having iced tea shot to the back of my head beside information like how to ride a bike. I pinched two Martini glasses and raised them.

"Dry?" I asked.

"Sweet and salty."

I mixed the libation with acumen achieved by turning around. "If you don't mind my due diligence, how'd you acquire access to my property?" I started walking back.

"Mr. Loam made an informal request to the manager."

Ah. She was trouble and made to look that way. "Do we have mutual interests?" I handed her a glass.

"To date."

I sat down on the edge of my green leather couch and took a deep sip of the cocktail. The oddness of the situation began to penetrate to the rational side of my head.

"Why did Loam send you, Andrea?"

"He wanted me to discuss options with you."

"Options for what? This isn't balancing out."

"It's junior, really. We'd like a summary of your meeting with city security this afternoon."

That one felt like a small slap. The questioning of my professional silence was an insult.

"Executive session," I said. "I'm quite sure Mr. Loam values confidentially."

"He values you, Mr. Kirst. Mr. Loam requested that I submit to you a contract for retention."

"Is he in need of additional service?"

"Not at this time."

"But he wants me on retainer." A tincture of annoyance crept into my voice. I hoped Andrea wouldn't believe it to be directed at her.

She uncrossed her legs and leaned forward. She let the Martini hang in her upturned hand. "He'll compensate with liquid assets for a memorandum of agreement."

It didn't take Loam a day of watching me to decide he didn't like what he saw. He thought I might break my oath and that worried him. I didn't want anything more to do with the guy. I absolutely didn't want more contracts, trails, strings, or obligations, despite the tastiness of the package and delivery service. Another sip of the Martini burned down my throat.

I thought carefully about my next statement. I didn't want the meaning to be lost or misconstrued. "All relationships between Arthur Loam and myself have expired. Future relationships will not be brought to the table."

Andrea's eyebrows arched, like I'd just shown her a clown tattoo on my ass.

"That is an unfortunate downturn," she said. "There is more profit in having Mr. Loam as a partner than a competitor."

"Please return the following message: I am under obligation to keep all contracted conferences confidential."

"It shall be in my report." She stood up. "I will quote your statement of obligation."

"Bull," I said, standing up and sticking out my hand.

"Bull." She set her drink down, stood, and shook my hand. Warm, supple skin over toned muscle. I did not want to let go.

"Pleasure, Mr. Kirst." She turned towards the door.

"Pleasure, Andrea," came out of me like a spirit.

She left.

"But enough about me," I grumbled after the door closed.

Had I not been so befuddled, and perhaps a tad flattered by the offer to join his criminal empire, maybe I would've been angry at the breaking and entering. The anger never came. Loam had three hundred ways of delivering his message, each easier, cheaper, and more legal. He wanted to communicate all kinds of things to me, all of which worked better without words.

But I like words.

I had no anger because I had realized something Loam may not have wanted to convey: he thought I could be bought. He thought I treated my oath — my license to facilitate conversations — like a drink coaster. He thought me self-serving and dishonorable because he thought that of everyone. That was his world view. Looking through it for a moment gave a speck of insight. I never did take him as a murder-for-passion kind of guy. He killed for enterprise.

He never should have corrected me about that burial ground. It made me think long, deep, and high about correcting him.

I walked over to the climate control pad. Andrea had changed the setting to Lilacs. I switched it back to Spring Rain and sat down to finish Andrea's drink.

Arthur Loam killed Paul Dombrowski and I couldn't tell anyone. Fair enough. Police business. His motives shouldn't matter to me any more than his shoe size. Loam killed for a reason though and that could sit outside our privileged conversations.

Let's start at the start, I said to myself.

"House, Sugarhill Gang," I said out loud. I settled into the comfy chair. "Play 'Rapper's Delight.'" I threw back the rest of the Martini as the house stereo whipped up. The saccharine smell of lilacs washed away in the gentle rain.

Chapter 6

From "Tales without Interpreters"
The optician was sick of sinking money into renovating his old home. He asked the plumbing contractor for a fully itemized estimate. At the line for "sweating" he becomes furious. They honestly thought they could get away with that? "I can perspire myself, thank you very much." He crosses it out. The plumbers shrug, finish and leave. The pipes pour seventy-five gallons of water into his basement before he finds the main shut off.

I was being followed. I was sure of it. Well, almost sure. My senses had ramped up in the last few hours and were now at fieldmouse level. I heard hoots and hisses everywhere. Awareness of my paranoia did nothing to depreciate it. A black Monte Carlo cruised two cars behind me since I'd left my apartment that evening. Sure, it could have been someone going my way. At any other point in my life, I would not have noticed it. Now, I noticed little else. I stared into the review mirror like an evil stepmother.

The night grew. I tried to distract myself with a search for a good adjective. *Tenebrous.* No wind. No moon. Just moist, palpable air. I would have been happy to leave the city if my destination hadn't been the suburbs. My oldest, oddest friend Larry Crep lived in a neighborhood north of Beau Fleuve. It took about twenty minutes to get there if everybody else wasn't trying to do the same thing. It was never a trip to be enjoyed. Once you're on the Thruway, there's nothing and no one to look at. Once you're in his hamlet, there's nothing but lawns, driveways, and kids. No single-man's land.

The Monte Carlo took the Thruway, too. Okay. It is how one gets out of the city. Lots of people use it, so many in fact that the state built the six lane, elevated highway. I calmed myself with that thought until the Monte Carlo took my exit. The car followed me, a steady two car lengths behind, until I reached Crep's street. Then it continued on alone. I exhaled. Maybe I wasn't being followed. There were probably twenty thousand homes off this stretch of highway, right? My Saab followed the track right up Crep's driveway and stopped behind his minivan. A patient blue, with wood on the side.

The lumbering clouds refused any starlight, but the dull glows of video monitors in the family rooms of the white trimmed houses of the suburb speckled the area. Quiet, low, long. I pressed the doorbell of the Crep's household. The neighborhood was so quiet I heard the chimes from inside and someone walk through the front hall.

"Will," Larry stood in the doorway, disappointingly unflustered.

"Larry."

"We're receiving." He opened the door. "Line in, line in." I looked up and down his street. I thought I saw a black car at the far end. No, I scolded myself. Bad imagination. Bad imagination. Down boy. "Thanks."

"Query your process, man?"

"Surge. You know. I do not go to fun."

He smiled. I smiled.

"Pro, Will." Ann greeted me with a hug and kiss. Larry's wife was a medical imagist, specializing in the lower back, and far too fetching to be married to him. It was no secret. I had told him more than a dozen times. They were one of those couples you see out — a lanky, balding slouch, and a dainty, luminous professional who should be starring in shampoo commercials — and you say to yourself, "What's she doing with him? He doesn't look that wealthy."

"What's the pathology? Benign?" Her tone had motherly concern. "I hope."

"Complications," I replied.

"Beer? Coffee?" she asked.

"Negative, but thank you."

"Merge. Merge." Larry waved me further into the home. The lights were dim because they had been watching one of those sitcoms where the kid takes the family car even though he's not old enough to drive and overhears her friend saying something out of context and the stupid dad thinks he's losing his job. They're less charming in Cyber, the predominate language in the Crep household. They had a comfortable, cluttered, lived-in home. An empty glass here, a thrown pillow there. Lunar Man toys strewn about. I refrained from dropping to the floor and playing with them, sticking to my mission with determination that would have made Lunar Man proud.

"Query the running, Larry?" I asked as we sat and Ann lilted into the kitchen.

"Looping, you?"

"Burnt and bugged. Therefore my line-up."

"Continue." He looked serious even though I tried to look flip.

"Require a file share," I said. "Requisite."

He scrunched his lips to the left side of his face to display mild displeasure with my request. "Query."

"Access. Maybe one byte. No more than a meg, really."

"Aw, Will…." He wasn't happy.

Ann came back into the room with three longneck Molson Canadians, caps off. "So, Will, condition?" she asked.

"Thanks." I took one. "All negative."

Despite the previous six hours, I hate to lie, even in phatic exchanges. Small talk is talk and that's my profession, so I try to maintain veracity at all times. It's not easy. As an interpreter you become aware of how much conversation is necessary and how much is just fill. Translate for a while, you come to understand that the majority of conversation is weather, superficial health, sports, and celebrity gossip. I didn't have the mood for prolonged niceties and good friends should allow one to be laconic on occasion. I turned back to Larry and lost my smile. "Meat run, Larry. Clear."

"Query access remote?"

I knew this part of the evening would present the biggest obstacle. If he wasn't pleased about dredging up some data for me, he really wasn't going to be pleased that he couldn't do it from his home. "Off. Line-up to your office." I tried to look like a shivering lamb. Pathetic. Vulnerable.

He took a swig of his beer and grinned as he swallowed. "You total surge, man."

"Wait," Ann said. "You both need to be ambulatory?"

Cyber not being her first language — though she had a fair understanding of the tongue, her job being a hybrid and her husband being Larry — she wanted to make sure she understood.

"A very quick visit." I swigged my beer.

Now Ann slid her lips to the side, showing displeasure she didn't want to annunciate. Crep said nothing. I smiled inside. My lack of disclosure intrigued him. He liked a mystery as much as I did. He could easily be coaxed into mischief. I gave a sweet good-bye to Ann and we were off.

———<>———

Based on my childhood, I'm not exactly sure how I came to be an interpreter. I spent my summers building/ fixing/altering scooters, computers, electronic toys, video monitors, and anything else my friend Larry Crep and I found in the garbage, attic, or basement. I picked up knowledge of electronics and physics and firstaid along the way, but Larry did the actual engineering. His family's shed served as our robot factory, jet-cycle shop, and Zeppelin hanger. The stuff of dreams. That last one nearly killed us. Being twelve we couldn't exactly go buy enough hydrogen to get off the ground. We could, however, generate lots of hydrogen with power and water. Enough to render that poor shed a smoldering memory.

Through high school all our stunts became silicon based. Larry went on to make a career of it. I went another way. Most interpreters will tell you computers are the enemy — algorithmic translation is the competition, after all — forgetting that processing power pretty much birthed our whole profession in the first place. Computers became the personal tailors of talk. First, people took in what they wanted — rocketry, knitting, finance, white supremacy. Then they adjusted their style — liberal, conservative, batshit crazy, backwards nutjob. Finally, the lingo took hold. If you're an architect, why get your news and entertainment dumbed down to the commonest of denominators? The architect gets their information in their terms, crowding out other words, phrases and idioms. Pretty soon that architect needs help understanding the developer requesting the twenty thousand square foot mixed use structure. And visa versa, though that was probably always the case going back to Imhotep.

Computers created interpreters, but as a stopgap. And we know it. Every day some new translation infostructure emerges, shaking off the slime of past faux pas. Every year the silicon brains evolve, getting better at nuance and context. Someday they'll win. And so we hate them. Except for the phone. That doesn't count. Or the house control.

Or my car, driving itself down the Thruway, so I could bring Larry up to speed, without telling him anything … inappropriate. He thought I led a wild, dashing, sex and alcohol-filled single life. Which allowed me to be vague. By not offering specifics I honored my oath and stoked his interest. Ah, the projected myths of the married. Always thinking the bed's bouncier in the one-bedroom loft.

"Your peripherals are what? Copper?" He laughed as he poked the buttons and knobs of the car stereo. He did not approve.

"The tone is tight," I protested.

"You need liquid monitors. Enhance the high end."

"Bass is priority. My content is vintage hip hop."

"I upgraded last week. I have two surplus, off line. I'll install."

"Flop. Reprioritize. High end the secondary parameter. Thanks."

"Hey. Query sat program?"

What are friends for? My buddy left his happy home in the middle of a work night to do something illegal for me just because I asked. Friends keep you out of trouble. Real friends keep you from getting into trouble alone.

My car stopped at the gates of Dataspan. Larry leaned over me and said his name and employee code into a small, glass circle on the side of the guard booth.

The gates parted without a sound, letting us into the parking lot of a seamless, five-story, shiny black cube. The first time I visited I couldn't even find the front entrance. I had to wait until someone emerged to get a bearing on the door. The building worked well for a business that hated people.

Regardless of the secrecy and security, the company was nothing more than an enormous information hub. Dataspan mapped and modeled, finding social patterns in social patters. Who collects anime. Who drives French bicycles. Who buys candy bars with black labels, who with white. That type of thing. Government jobs supposedly require the vault-like treatment — it's rumored that Dataspan can measure your tendency towards cheating on taxes by the kind of socks you buy — but in reality the building housed nothing a normal person could steal, or would want, which meant, I guess, that I'd stopped being normal.

We entered the foyer. Larry put his eyes on the peepholes for a retina scan. I had to thumb a plate on the wall. A fluorescent orange visitors patch curled out of a slot in the wall like a tongue. I stuck it to my lapel. Larry snapped on his ID badge and we were in.

We padded silently through dim halls to his tiny office. It's funny how you try to walk so quietly when there isn't anyone to hear you; I can't decide if it's an innate desire not to disturb what little peace one stumbles across in life or the acknowledgement of something lonely about the echoes of empty space.

I knew Larry did well for himself because he had an office. When he started this job, he sat on one of the benches, staring at his section of the twenty-five-foot-long ribbon monitor. Pigs at a trough. They'd cram ten or twelve programmers on a stretch of wood, strap gear and goggles on their heads, and make them dive into swill. The farmers strolled back and forth behind them, using their old-fashioned eyes to make sure their stock stayed on task.

As he skipped behind his desk and put on an eyepiece, I could tell Larry had some measure of pride in his place, but he didn't want to waste time with the one-byte tour. He wanted to get on with it. If he had any apprehensions about breaking company policy — perhaps an actual law or two — he didn't let them show. Three different monitors surrounded his desk. One small, blue one came up from the desktop. A meter of amber stretched across two curvy vines swinging down from the ceiling. A cookie-sheet-sized monitor clung to the left wall, reminding me of an unfinished mercurial painting from the early days of the Art Techno movement. They all lit up in unison. He briefly looked at each monitor, letting the laser from his eyepiece invoke an arcane spell. He leaned over his desk and looked at me, waiting for my instruction. I couldn't truly feel the laser's dot on my upper left cheek, but it tickled nonetheless. That sense of being a target. It's itchy. It's probably one of the reasons privacy laws exist, as in the ones I was about to break.

"Query file 'Arthur Loam.' No trace and no parameters," I said.

"No parameters?" Larry frowned at me. He knew that to be impossible. "Off. Total. Zero code to enable. No structure. Programs access data by parameter. Example: 'boat owners.' No channel to specified entry. Query?"

"Loam is ... buggy. Intermittent error. No code."

"Inadequate input. Search...." Even as he said he couldn't, I could tell he contemplated a way that he could.

Larry eyed the amber screen, swishing the laser back and forth, occasionally speaking into his headset, and occasionally speaking out at me. Usually something not so nice. He tapped on his hand pad and bobbed his head a lot and made faces.

The problem, as I understood it, was that Dataspan specialized in organizing broad psychographic information. If I wanted to know how many tennis fans in the greater Beau Fleuve area had purchased Westinghouse refrigerators last June, all I had to do was ask. That was easy. If I wanted to know everything about a specific tennis fan, I'd have to ask them personally. Anything else was very far from the usual request and getting close to being against the law. Advertising agencies, chain restaurants, and the US Department of Information cared less about one person than they cared about everyone. Big numbers dictated Dataspan's structure. Conspiracy specialists are free to disagree. Especially because Larry could run the system backwards.

But could he do it without anyone ever knowing?

I sat there and listened to the plastic hitting plastic and Larry mumbling and knew that Larry would find a way to weave through the structure. For the magician's first trick, he made an hour disappear.

The red laser projecting from the right of Larry's eye piece swooped noiselessly from screen to screen. By the speed at which Larry moved, I knew he had gone from thinking to concocting a strange enchantment to summon my data. He began to allow a pinch of a grin. I allowed my eyes to close.

"Will. Stay up. User input requisite." My head snapped up.

"Query Queue?"

"Beta run on the line, bug scan queued, if operable then go to net and run."

I scootched up to the desk and planted my elbows. I looked at the pretty colors on the monitor in a vain attempt to extract a clue as to what might be transpiring. Larry certainly made it sound like something good bubbled in his brew.

"Base match run. Code search choice files for 'Loam, Arthur' entries, Beau Fleuve ADI. Establish new file, 'Loam' only entries." He seemed quite pleased with himself.

When the glyphs on the wall screen changed, Larry laughed a little and clapped his hands. He pounded some more commands into his pad and then sat back, putting his hands behind his head.

"Run clear, man. Juiced and enabled." He tilted towards me, satisfied and spirited.

"Run time?" I asked.

"Twelve minutes."

"Query?" Wasn't that like three years in computer time? You never saw international jewel thieves sit around after they've palmed the royal sapphire.

"Coffee on the line," Larry said.

"Server up. Let's line."

Our walk to the coffee machine caused more noise than our previous stroll. Larry loved cutting through the supposedly insuperable and couldn't help but talk about it. He explained his data search: parameters so narrow as to only find 'Loam, Arthur.' He didn't care for the time it might take, but the search used everything as its source. Everything. School records from Tibetan monasteries. Cigar wrapper efficacy tests. Slide-rule collector buddy lists. It dumped into several locations, to be picked up by another seemingly unrelated program, thus confusing any trace. When complete we would have a complete dossier on Loam, Arthur. We got off lucky, only having to wait twelve minutes.

A blue-green laser swept my chest. My face went cartoony, I fumbled my coffee, and may have made a slight "eawh" kind of noise. A black plastic tank the size of a milk carton pointed its turret at Larry.

"Hardware defense?" I asked.

Larry shook his head. "Buggy, Will."

"Spiked day."

"Mr. Crep." A large, human male in a blue uniform stood in the doorway to the breakroom, the small tank at his side like a dog. "And guest."

"Hi," Larry said, squeezing a smile from a face that wanted to go a different way.

"Your purpose at the scene?" he asked me. "Query office session?" the voxbox on his shoulder echoed.

I smiled and waved my hand around as if washing woodwork. "You can stow the squawker. We got a channel."

"Ah." The security guard tapped his belt. "You on the job?"

"Mouthpiece."

"Swell." Interpreters were not as impressive as cops — to this guy, anyway. To most, really, who am I kidding. "Curfew violation. No off-the-books partners after seven p.m."

"I'm sorry—" Larry started.

"Guilty." I stopped him. "I coerced Mr. Crep into said violation. A little side-job. Background check on a female, redhead, midtwenties, one hundred and twenty pounds, and single, who's number escaped me."

"I'm not—" the guard began.

"Just a number," I pleaded. "I need to reach out to her."

He stared at us for three, slow blinks. Then he shook his head. "Roger that." He backed out of the doorway and put his hands over his eyes. "I'm looking the other way for five minutes. Heel, Cooper."

The small tank rolled after him.

Back in Larry's office, Larry fluttered his hands before the monitors. The screens sparkled with text. He grinned, took my phone, and slid the file he'd conjured on board. I glanced at his screen while it loaded. No milk or toothpaste like you'd expect. It's interesting how little rich people actually buy, as if everything's all there for them, all the time. 'Tuscarora Indian Reservation' caught my eye. It sat at the top of Loam's activity list, which made sense. That's what he did today. He leased a Zeppelin tower on the Reservation. I had not realized the address of his new parcel put it on Tuscarora land. The next few entries, working back through the summer, read much the same. His estivation was composed of buying and borrowing and buying and borrowing.

"Would you ever add a site on the Reservation," I asked Larry — and myself.

"Can I?" he scoffed. "Solid firewall. Unstable lines in, unstable lines out, right?"

He had a point. Sovereign land isn't simply available to the average joe. "No value is the same for all users," I said. "But you're correct. My data says the place is protected."

"Not protected," Larry said. "Compromised. Fried to brick. Once a place is off-line like that, it never comes back."

Yes, parts of Niagara County were uninhabitable. There was a Quarantine Zone. And there was Tuscarora land. Because I never cared, I never set them next to each other in my mind.

Larry tapped the screen I'd been reading. It went blank. "Big data. Not secure. I relay this to you thinking it will ping nothing, but. Big but. Data grows to insecurity. Can you acquire that?"

"Data grows to insecurity," I repeated. Repeating is, after all, what I do.

Chapter 7

From "Tales without Interpreters"
The bond trader leans back in the chair. The dentist smiles, bringing a mask close to the trader's face. "I'm going to put you under," the dentist says. The bond trader panics, knocks the mask away and runs, tooth aching all the way.

A nine-inch mulberry tree was the closest thing to a pet I could allow myself. I'm fully capable of loving hamsters and Dachshunds and turtles and such, but any animalia other than me wouldn't last five days in my apartment. The bonsai only survived by virtue of the mineral-monitoring, auto-rotating, light-sensitive planter in which the tree sat. Connected right to the water line, I never had to give the tree anything — the planter even did the trimming! — which worked out well for both of us. Other than the tree, my bedroom looked like a human garage.

Propped against the headboard, staring at the bonsai, I twirled my phone through my fingers. I tossed it up a few feet, caught it and twirled it some more. Anything to keep from using it as intended. I didn't want its help. I'm not cyberphobic. I've got the average one hundred and thirty-four intelligent devices in my home just like any other young, American professional. It's just....

I'm about twelve or so and I bring my computer out to the porch to sit with mom. She had her twelve-string Ovation-made guitar on her lap, lazily strumming out chords. I'd been fiddling with the music programs on the computer and decided to play along with her. I called up a bass program and she snapped the screen down nearly nipping my fingers.

"You want to play the bass line I'll go up in the attic and find you a bass and teach you how to play."

"But I can type—"

"That ain't music. That's sand rustling in sandbox. I don't play with sandboxes."

I just looked at her. She had never spoken to me this way before.

"I was just having fun."

"Sometimes one kind of fun kills off another. No son of mine is going to help dig the grave."

The whole exchange has been buried in me ever since, not deceased, but undead, rising from its cranial crypt at wrong moments, refusing any exorcism I try.

A few years after that, I learned that my parents met in a dump of a bar. Her band played there twice a month. They covered old music and sang the lyrics in English. Over the years the audiences shrunk until it was only my mom and dad having a drink, trying to ignore the hyper-thumping, never repeating AI jazz that grew like kudzu, choking off the other harmonies of public spaces. Not too many people spoke core English, even fewer wanted to listen to its songs.

Mom and dad got married. She got a real job, some kids, a house, and all the happiness she could harness despite putting her first love on a hook in the back of a closet.

"Computers," she said one Christmas, plucking "Silent Night" out on her Ovation. "They make it sooooo easy."

I looked down at the spanking-new interface suit I had just opened. Santa only brought it because I had been so dreadful.

"Messages coming to you in any dialect. That just ain't right." She continued to play.

"Computers aren't to blame." My sister looked up from her scenter set. "It's big business. They're the ones." Her rebel years had begun. But only just. She'd spend the rest of her day using her new toy to concoct her own, personalize perfumes.

"They teach you that in school?"

"No. I've been reading Dad's books. Bankers become Investment Bankers, then Biotech Investment Bankers, then

Audio Bioelectric Foreign Investment Bankers or some such thing. People have become so specialized they can't help but learn hardly anything besides their jobs. Big Business pounded people into their holes."

"The computer was the hammer they used."

Mom played a chord but it wasn't the right one. She left the unresolved sound linger.

Deciding to become an interpreter popped a pressure valve in me. I'd escaped the fate of those kids who didn't want to be actuaries like their fathers and their father's fathers, despite the fact that they only spoke Math and Risk. Or worse, those who didn't know what they wanted to be at all, regardless of the tongues spoken in their homes. Still, the pressure resumed, as I came to realize the heat is always on. Hotter for some, indirect and uneven for others, but always growing. The field of communication facilitation is cool, but no refuge.

Interpreters hold a tentative place in society. We fill a gap until machine intelligence evolves to the point in which it can translate the totality of human conversation. Human interpreters don't always get it right, but we're real good at backing up, doing over, or correcting communication by other means. It's still a good part art. Once the software is smart enough to pick up the subtleties and indexical meanings that turn words into utterances, interpreters will all join the ranks of bookbinders, typesetters, and mailmen. So, I have an uneasy relationship with phones because they're the young kids coming up, itching to boost me from my job. I hate them because they're so charming and helpful.

Sometimes one kind of smart kills off another.

I set my phone into my sandbox, which did whatever it had to do to connect with the rest of the house. A silent, invisible language I had nothing to do with. The bedroom wall south of my bed flicked on. It blinded me for a second. I'd become used to the lack of light. I took the knob of the door to the universe and asked it to open up on the Tuscarora Nation.

I've lived less than twenty miles from the Reservation my whole life. I have never visited the place. Not knowingly at least. There are no fences or lookout towers. One could drive right through it without ever realizing they'd crossed, in a legal sense, in and out of another nation. The computer had to tell me the where and what of the Rez. My ignorance as wide as the open plains.

In 1803 the US government gave (gave back?) the Tuscarora people a nine-point-three square mile rectangle of land north-east of Niagara Falls. About a hundred and fifty years later, they'd take back a chunk for a water reservoir, flipping the phrase *Indian giver* into ironical irrelevance. The reservoir allowed Niagara Falls' hydro-generators to keep sparking out electricity at a consistent rate. Energy rules and renewable energy rules absolutely.

The remaining parcel lays as a sovereign nation. The Tuscarora own it, as one might a letterman jacket from high school. They did not have any use for it, nor could they give it up. What had once been arable corn fields, strawberry patches, and rows and rows of grapes had gone sour. No one worked the land anymore. No one lived on the land. One of the many byproducts of cheap hydroelectricity is power-hungry industry: chemical production, batteries, data-mining and storage. One of the byproducts of industry is reckless greed. Benzoyl chlorides left to leech with languor into the land. Electrolytes hoisted into the air by neglect, pulled down by ever vigilant gravity to soak soil into uninhabitability. Much of the Tuscarora territory and surrounding area is irrevocably contaminated. A Zeppelin tower lease on the Rez was a sandbox in the Sahara. The old kind of sandbox, not the new kind. The new kind is probably helpful. So my metaphor didn't make a ton of sense.

Which led me back to Loam. He made more money than sense. He knew something I didn't. I believed this to be a mathematical certainty. I knew so little about so much. I had a great deal of exposure to lots of facts and knowledge and goings-on, but in the end, I talked to people for a living using other people's words. I could feel my ignorance all over me, an odor clinging to my skin. Loam could correct me on the variances of burial sites because I'd given him the chance. I would not let that happen again.

The Loam file Larry gave me transferred from my phone to my home frame. I told the machine to display it all. The datalogical version of Niagara Falls appeared on my wall. Larry had been right. Of the myriad ways I could have consumed this information, I'd picked the worst of the worst. In want of a sip, I had tapped into an eight-hundred-thousand-gallon-per-second gush.

Of the many silly, money-milking courses forced on me in college, Field Facilitation was the most surprising. I had expected a semester of useless communication theory and ended with bag of tricks. For instance, because not all interpretation takes place in the organized quiet of a conference room, we spent weeks studying selective auditory attention. The Cocktail Party Effect. Most people have the ability to hear their name through the cacophony of a crowd. Or tune to a single voice in a room of talkers, which is the handy part. While the phenomenon is not completely understood, we can learn techniques for strengthening the ability. It helps interrupters work streetside at a murder scene, amongst other things. And it made me think about focus and sorting and pulling that lone, loathsome weed from lush bluegrass lawn.

Loam's new tower. That arrogant dandelion in a hump of hydrangea. I told the computer to show me recent financial transactions, sorted backwards. So it did.

Loam had recently picked up four other Zeppelin towers. Not enough to corner the market or send up a flare for the Federal Trade Commission, Federal Aviation Administration, Fish and Wildlife, The Bureau of Indian Affairs ... I couldn't think of anyone who'd care. Except for me.

And I shouldn't have. I should've brought up a recent issue from one of the twenty-two journals to which I subscribed and ignored, read a piece by one of my esteemed colleagues on pragmatics or cognitive barriers and fallen into sweet, sweet sleep. Instead, I looked at Loam's loops of friends, social contacts, boards, clubs and affinities. He gave to the arts, the local children's hospital and ten different political campaigns. Five conservative, five liberal, all at the county and state level. Right down middle. You could call this fair, or smart business, or the results of being on no side but your own.

The cursor on my screen jumped a line.

I shot up like a catapult, like my body wanted to launch my face at the wall. I had not ordered the computer to do anything. Sadly, no one else in my bedroom told my computer to do anything either. No one leaned over and pouted, "William, dear, don't we have something better to do than look at these silly old spread sheets?"

I killed the frame and ripped my phone from the sandbox. Someone, somewhere had tagged the data. He or she or they were curious about who might be curious about Arthur Loam. Now they might be highly curious about me. Great. If there's one thing snoops really hate, it's another snoop.

A need to call Crep shot through my mind at light speed. I flicked that thought off. I'd try to keep him in the shadows. If I could. I'd asked Larry for so much data that millions of lines of code could be lurking in the hall. I knew my system had an acceptable level of security. Larry had set it up. But none of the protections worked if I brought the data tag in from my side of the wall.

Dumb, dumb, dumb — he had warned me. I could've grabbed anything in that data sweep. Now I felt naked, with no curtains in a glass room. And I felt exhausted. And too addled to do anything about it.

Other than hit the big, red button. Larry had installed the kill switch because of my job — I inevitably encountered secrets. The red button disconnected me from the outside world.

So now I could add *alone* to naked and beat.

If you're having girl problems, I feel bad for you son.

I got ninety-nine problems, but—

Oh, Jay Z. Feel bad for me, son. I've got a hundred problems, because I'm my own bitch.

Chapter 8

From "Tales without Interpreters"
A doctor wants to buy her husband a wristwatch for their anniversary. She knows the type of ornate antique he likes and points to one in the dealer's case. The dealer takes it out and tells her it has a number of complications. "Oh," she says. "How about the one next to it?" He informs her that it also has several complications. "And that one in back?" "Just one complication," the dealer says. Frustrated, the doctor asks if all these watches have complications? To which the dealer replies yes, all of them. The doctor leaves, wondering how the place can stay in business. She buys her husband cufflinks.

Keeping my mind on work was eating soup with a chop-stick. One, singular. I caught some of the big stuff, but most of the day drained away before I got a taste. Then one of my spicier clients, Chapman Sadabahar, came in so I could help him talk to his accountant. Chapman had a few years on me. He'd recently grown his hair — top, down the sides, across the chin — making his actual age tough to figure. Round and milky, he never appeared to have too much energy. Until he determined you were worthy of seeing his mania. The criteria for worthiness remained classified — intelligence, necessity, you didn't try to con, play, or ply him, a mixture of all those and others? I never knew. He liked me, so I liked him.

Due to my distractions, the twenty-minute job took me sixty and I think he wrote off a llama named Trip, as opposed to a trip to Lima, on his taxes. Chapman ran records management for a drayage company through a bank whose name I couldn't hope to remember because they all buy each other up and hyphenate their names more often than I floss. No one at his company spoke his Transpo-drayage-finance sub-sub-dialect, so he spent most of his time actually working ... until he got my ear. Meeting with me knocked the big nut off a verbal fire hydrant. He talked and talked and talked to me because he could. Once we finished the formal meeting, and the accountant left, I prepared for the deluge.

Although this time, I would try to direct the flood.

"Drayage," I said. "Carting goods around."

"My stock-in-trade," Chapman said back.

"You use a ton of Zeppelins?"

"Blimps, dirigibles, various classes and sizes. LTAs — Lighter Than Air — the way we book."

"Off the books, if you don't mind...."

"Naw." He made a little 'n' with his mouth and leaned forward. "Dump."

"Why would anyone want an LTA dock on the Tuscarora Reservation, in the Quarantine Zone?"

"That tract of land in DD from IAG?"

DD meant driving distance. IAG was ... I didn't know, so I said "yes" and hoped it didn't matter.

"No one," Chapman said. "That's why there ain't one."

"Now there is," I said.

"That's restricted area, or at the very least stacked so tight it don't matter. Empty."

"Cleared to dock."

Chapman scrutinized me, comfortable enough to show his puzzlement. "You know a party what built a spike in a no go?"

Spike. Slang for a Zeppelin tower. Right. "A refurb of a legacy. Would a receiver surface?" I asked.

"Prospective," Chapman said. "I will report this with caution. The first thing you log in my business is no hold goes unfilled. An anecdotal here: NYC takes in everything. A big compactor of a port, right? Zero manufacturing base and yet we never book out light. Never. Every belly outbound is maxed with recyclables. Goods in, waste out, we take a vig either way. A specification of beauty. There is always some commodity at some rate to book. You give me a point A and there'll be a point B what wants to ship there."

"So," I tried out, "one could profit from a dock, any dock, even in Quarantine?"

"There is an asshole for every seat, if you can match my understanding."

"But this spike's near nothing?"

"This is not in my wheelhouse, but affirmative. The spike's got no feed, as in you can't belly up. The spike's got no draw, as in no one has ever requested that as a destination. At least not through me. There's no one there to want anything. There's no one there to book anything out. I'd have to check in with Reg, but I'm set on there's no legal haul out. Empty as suck, Will. Empty as suck."

"That was my assessment," I replied. "You know, as a civilian."

"As a civy, I will deliver you this: We have an old SOP in the business."

"A standard operating procedure." I looked for agreement.

"Yes," Chapman said. "The SOP is you can't get ahead with both eyes on the rearview mirror."

I nodded.

"The winds always change," Chapman said. "The green-ass liberals got their flag over the house and senate for at least another two years. That don't mean it's always going to point the same way."

"You track politics?"

"Tracking blowhards is mandatory. Same as the weather. Rights-of-way, permissions, regs or hurricanes, tailwinds and dry spells. It's homologous. What causes course corrections requests my homologous attention."

"Homologous?"

"All the same," Chapman said. "When your whole hull is filled with just one kind of thing."

"Yours is filled with weather and politics," I said.

Chapman chuckled. "Waste and what-not. Weight, space, time, and money. It's all the same to me."

"You're an interesting man, Chapman."

"A sundry," he said. "I declare myself to be a living, breathing sundry. Alert, Will. I don't log what you've got going to the Zone or the origin of the question, but it makes you a bit of a sundry yourself. Nothing bad about that. Until there is."

"Thank you." I smiled. Clients never called me interesting. Some interpreters may have taken it as an insult, our goal being to be invisible and all. Not me.

Chapman left. I checked my messages. Bremburg again. Yesterday, I would've found it spooky that the cops wanted to talk to me. Today, I progressed to annoyed. I'd spent my time in the nutcracker. I didn't split. It didn't seem fair that they got to try to snack on me again so soon.

I drove over listening to N.W.A.

In the station house, I watched two plain-clothed police officers tow a kid, around twenty I guessed, by a clear leash wrapped around his wrists, up through his crotch and over his shoulder. Any attempt to run would have spun him like a top. They lead him through an obstacle course of desks and half walls and uninterested others.

"You a missionman?" the first cop spat. Female, with the thickness and confidence of someone who knew they could flip you twice before you realized this wasn't some Kung Fu film.

"Kay?"

"Crap out," she said. "You a missionman?"

I'd never heard the phrase before. It made the whole trip worth it. I love hearing street lingo so fresh it hasn't been vacuumed up by the posters yet. It made me feel ahead, even if I never had use for the phrase.

"No, Betty. I got no mission."

"Tong Kiev did not paper you?"

The other cop, a male about my age, stood behind the kid on the leash, well into his personal space.

"Tong? What that some fancy panty?"

The female officer yanked the cord and male cop fished a slip of paper out of the kid's left front pocket.

"Hey," the male cop said. "Look what fell out your pants."

"Not on my person," the kid shouted.

"I balled it."

"Not on my person," he shouted again. "I want a kit. I'm exercising my rights to a kit."

The use of the word *exercising* made me smile. I enjoyed hearing people mix all kinds of argots when pressed. He'd been around lawyers just enough to get it right. The terms *paper* and *missionman* intrigued me. I'm thinking he ran messages for someone who didn't trust the privacy of electronic communication. He gave paper messages to employees and sent them on missions. I needed to hear more to be sure.

That didn't happen. Bremburg emerged from his office and motioned me in.

A woman sat in front of his desk, perched on the edge of her chair, legs and arms pressed tight together. She could have been carved from a single log. Her eyes were pink pillows, her hair oaken straw. Had this been a holding cell or interrogation room I would have assumed she'd been Maced during her apprehension.

"Mr. Kirst, meet Olivia Carl." Bremburg sat behind his desk.

"Nice to meet with you," I said in the most general way, and I sat down.

"I need a mouthpiece," Bremburg said. "You okay with this?"

"If I can assist, I will." I turned to the woman. Midthirties, fit but drawn, probably pretty on any other day. "Your tongue, Ms. Carl?"

"Mixed," she said. "Merc and AC."

Merchant and Arts-and-Crafts. Not an unusual combination. Being called to police headquarters for a question and answer, that counted as queer.

"Affirmative," I said to Bremburg. "Over."

Bremburg gave me the slightest of smiles and looked at Olivia. "Can you relate to me relevant facts as regards your father?"

"Inventory the features of your father that might interest me," I said.

She looked at me, then at officer Bremburg. She pushed her lower lip against her upper, as a baby might, getting ready for her first word. "Broken."

I didn't think to translate that word. We three sat in silence for a moment.

Bremburg eased his voice to barely audible. "Your father's residence?"

"His space?" I asked.

"Legally speaking, he lives with me, but he hasn't been inside in months."

I turned to Bremburg. "Subject is vagrant." I waited for him to nod, because what he heard — the word *inside* — had a substantially different meaning in copland.

"The motivation for the vagrancy?" he asked.

"Why is he on the street?" I asked Olivia.

"I'm unsure," Olivia said. "Since Mom passed, Dad ... darkened. It's like the lights went out. One by one. He wanted to ... I'm unsure ... close up?"

I had to pause, resort to the metaphor, guess as to what Bremburg needed. "Wife deceased. Husband takes it bad. Starts to give up."

"Give up?" Bremburg repeated.

"Psychologically," I clarified.

"He ever have a psych eval?"

"Has your father had a mental health inspection?"

"Three," Olivia stated. "He never earned a space at the hospital. Not broken enough, they always say."

I looked at Bremburg and he waved me off. He got the gist of what Olivia had said. More than that. I think he knew it all already.

"We found traces of gunpowder on your father. He always possess a gun?"

"A gun? Like with bullets?" Olivia skipped me.

Bremburg nodded.

"Never," Olivia said. "Not his oeuvre. No talent. He took space on the street because he did not want to add to my overhead or my sister's. Nobody's."

"Negative," I relayed. "The subject in question had no knowledge of, or skill with, firearms. He chose vagrancy so as not to burden his relations."

"Violent tendencies?"

"Was your father damaging or destructive to property, persons or merchandise?"

"No," Olivia whined. "Don't you get it? Since Mom expired, he's wanted to fade. Recede into the background. He refused to sell himself into anyone's life."

"No history of violence. His current MO is full pull back. He's resistant to confrontation."

"Thank you very much, Ms. Carl." Bremburg rose.

I stood. Olivia stood. "Really, inspector. You've not made your best selection."

"Thank you again."

We watched her go. I didn't follow her out. I closed the door and spun to face Bremburg, who didn't look at all surprised.

"What's the deal?" I asked.

"What?"

"You needed a mouthpiece for that face-to-face?"

"You are assisting an investigation."

"Who's the father?"

"Phelan Carl. The guy we've arrested for the murder of Paul Dombrowski."

Bremburg watched my face like a classroom clock on the last day of school. He got what he wanted. Even if I wanted to, I couldn't have hidden my shock.

"Old skell," he said. "Homeless. Met Loam's description and tested positive for GPR. Tight case. He'll live the rest of his life in state prison, as a rag doll for some other skell."

"Right," I said, to Bremburg and to myself. He wanted me to meet the daughter. Hear her story. Visualize the tragedy about to unfold. We both knew Phelan Carl had nothing to do with the murder and that he wasn't a skell — a lowlife, a leech. We both knew who did, but like politics and religion, it was something we wouldn't talk about.

"I'm glad to have been of service," I said as I turned to leave.

"I'll reach out to you again," Bremburg said to my back, with neither threat nor creepiness. A simple statement of fact.

Chapter 9

From "Tales without Interpreters"
A man steps in the confessional and kneels facing the
screen between himself and the Catholic priest sitting
silently on the other side. "How long has it been since
your last reconciliation?" the priest asks. The man's
mouth falls open. "Father," he replies. "How did you even
know I was an accountant?"

A punched-out, dipping sun sprayed fiesta colors over downtown's glass and steel. I should have taken in the moment.
I try to be the stop-and-smell type. I did the stopping part,
next to my car, outside the police station. That meeting with
Bremburg and Olivia Carl, though — it didn't leave me open
for a lot of savoring. Reflecting, yes. Relishing, no. A tragedy
of a guy with a loving daughter, on his way to prison, because
Loam had framed him. The fact wouldn't digest — a ghost
pepper in my belly, burning and bubbling.

My word.

Sacrosanct communication plays an important role in
society. People need to feel they can speak freely, or they won't
speak at all. This is the only point of view an interpreter is
allowed. What I wanted was to walk back to the precinct house
and tell Bremburg everything. The plan had its advantages.
Justice, my peace of mind, maybe I'd help put a criminal in
prison. The plan also left me without a job, for which I'd spent
four years training for, at a cost of … I didn't want to perform
that calculation —not in dollars, and not in chips at the rock
on which society stands. The first trust. The word.

People don't like interpreters who no longer interpret.
They figure you either couldn't hack it — you couldn't listen

to other people talk, and then talk some yourself, how hard could that be, right? — or, you screwed up. Badly. Like you started a war, bankrupted an industry, or had a woman's kidney removed instead of her spleen. No one ever believed an interpreter simply wanted to *explore new horizons.*

Because it was never true.

I had to try something else. Not a new profession. I needed a new strategy within my current one. Another tack, a deeper review. Bremburg stopped short of saying that to me. He respected me and my oath, unlike some of my other recent acquaintances. The respect needed to be reciprocated.

For a second time, I thought about re-entering the precinct house.

My phone jiggled. "Who?" I whispered to the device.

"Kai."

"Accept." I heard the click. "Word," I said in full voice.

"Up," he returned. "The phone's telling me you're not too far."

"We'll always be close," I replied. Damn it. Why didn't I turn the friend-circle crap off? Like last night's game of virtual tag didn't generate enough terror. Having my house computer invaded, being followed, women breaking into my apartment. I had plenty of latent talent for paranoia, but I didn't feel like practicing.

"I've got two tickets to the Bisons' game."

"The game, as in the one that starts now."

"And the seats are good."

"So, you called me to brag."

"I'm sending one to your phone right now," Kai said. "Get here, get beer, and get social."

He hung up.

My decision had been made for me. Bremburg could do his job without me for a while longer. I got in my car, told it to take me to the ballpark and play something appropriate.

You know how we do, Roc-a-Fella forever, Jay Z hollered through my radio. The car stereo's intelligence chose a song that dealt with driving performed by the top artist on my list. Handy, but creepy. A song called "Politics as Usual." Which felt even creepier at the moment, what with my bicameral lobes' internal, personal politics. I laughed to myself — No, I laughed at myself — while Jay Z spilled about *skatin' through the town and puttin' it down.* I took his advice, leaving the police and interpreting and everyone else's troubles behind me. At least physically.

I couldn't clear my head. Bremburg kept creeping back in — a hook in a song you don't even like and yet hear on a continuous loop in your mind. The kind that seeps through you despite your resistance. Repeating. Repeating. Cops and their ploys. And to think, it's interpreters that get the bad rap.

And we do. Some people are weary of ex-interpreters, some are even more weary of the extant ones. As with psychologists — and I just added, cops — people are not always comfortable around those they perceive to have insight. Not general perceptiveness, but the intimate type. Does the shrink know I hate pistachio pudding because of my mother issues? Does the cop really suspect I might break into my brother-in-law's house to get my lawn-trimmer back? Does William Kirst think I can't appreciate this music because I only speak Juris? I cannot think outside my jury box? As if I'm locked into a language, and thereby locked out of the others? Maybe hip hop just sucks, Will. Maybe misogyny and materialism are not my gin and juice, Will

Isla's voice made the closing statements. A year-old echo. I digress.

The fringes of the linguistic community have not helped to quell this fear of insight. There is a faction who believes languages program thought, not the other way around. The Sapir-Whorf hypothesis of linguistic relativity. Learn Econ sub-English, you start to think like an economist. By corollary, if you know someone's verbal patterns, you can make assumptions about that person's thoughts. You can see into their minds. If a person speaks Econ, you can expect them to think in terms of supply and demand. You can make predictions. In a conversation about the price of leather, you say, "I know what you're going to say. Switch to silk." If you're not wearing a top hat and cape, people don't care for this kind of trick.

Interpreters don't play parlor games. The fear is bullshit. Except ... what did Chapman say? Until it isn't?

I once dated a woman who had studied art history. One of our dates took us through a local gallery. I'm staring at this big circle on the wall, and she starts telling me how it's a round peg in a square hole, how the artist is fighting the confines of art, expression, and society. And I'm seeing a large period. To me, it was punctuation. Not the beginning of a thought, but the end. When you work in words, words are your world. You don't have to be an interpreter all that long to see a similar effect in other professionals.

Marketers see in watercolor grays. Engineers in stark black and white. Doctors talk in scales, scientists in possibilities and probabilities. There are patterns, bigoted as it may sound. Recognizing these patterns is a form of insight, just shy of prejudice. For the most part, most of us, most of the time, have no use for such a penetrative conjecture. What's the point? It's rude and, well....

It's like that weird-shaped wrench you got from your grandfather. The one that's been stuck to the bottom of your toolbox since your first apartment. It will have a use one day. I decided to pull out that weird tool.

Chapman spoke Transpo but had an interest in politics. That made for an interesting mind. His use of the colloquialism *green-ass liberals* changed the indexical sphere of our exchange, creating an implicature, a meaning beyond his words. He put his ideas in the context of a more expansive group. Hard-ass conservatives and green-ass liberals. By giving a political description in place of a physical or scientific response, had he been signifying a greater issue? Politics at play on the Reservation? Loam could profit from that, maybe, somehow. Was that being discussed in circles I never entered? There were plenty of those.

I needed to expand my circles. I needed to think bigger and wider. Learn more. Do more.

A stoplight held me. The car in the lane next to me was a Duesenberg XJ. Long, dark, and glossy. It had rolling fenders, the ultimate in showing off. Look how much power I can afford to waste on the wind. I tried to peek inside the opaque windows. I couldn't see the gel seats, liquid speakers, and wet bar I'd read about. New luxury. My generation has watched a fat financial boom in this region. Back when this city was called Buffalo, one of these cars would have been as rare as, well, a wild buffalo. Now the herd was thick.

A reason for Beau Fleuve's renaissance, oddly enough, as I understood it, was the Niagara Falls Quarantine Zone. The nation's largest environmental disaster. In the last quarter century, my hometown became an international center for research into environmentally triggered diseases. Funds, grants, smart people — the medical professionals and scientists gathered at the watering hole, followed by pastry chefs, philosophers, actors, anthropologists, and artisanal ketchup makers setting up shop next to the handcrafted gherkins, doilies, candles, and petals pressed paper. Our art galleries teem with conversation starters. The Philharmonic is ranked fifth in the world. Top jazz musicians put Beau Fleuve on the tour, great ballplayers don't mind the trade. The general level of the brusque and haughty — and your chances of being viewed down a nose — has also escalated, but nobody charts that stuff. There is no snooty index. There is only boom or bust measured in money.

Local politicians counterclaim that Beau Fleuve has had fresh water, beautiful architecture, and people feeding the growth spurt. Those things are true, but like most things, they're part of a bigger thing. The world's leading cancer researchers did not settle a couple of miles outside of the Zone because of the beaches.

The City Council voted to change the name of the city about twenty years ago. I remember because there were huge parties, but it wasn't Christmas. To an eight-year-old it made little sense. They changed my hometown's name from something I could say — something I could actually draw on a good day — to something sounding like a muffled burp. The city officials didn't share my view. They thought the new name — which to make matters even more confusing was supposedly the original name hundreds of years ago — fit the new image of the city. Sophisticated. Stylish. Soon almost all signs of the fat, shaggy animal had been stripped away.

A sad repetition of history as the newly settled colonizers slaughtered the beast to force the Indigenous populations west. Buffalo became a mistake of history. Beau Fleuve could be mistaken for a decent Chardonnay. Our baseball team remained the Bisons. They are pennant contenders this year. Things could have gone worse.

A black Monte Carlo followed five cars behind me.

Chapter 10

From "Tales without Interpreters"
The building manager hired an arborist to put up a
Christmas tree. The forty-foot spruce filled the main hall
with stature and grace. The building manager gazed
upward, smiled and said, "Perfect. Let's trim it." He went
off to retrieve some boxes. The arborist thought the guy
was nuts, but went about his work. The building manager
soon returned, saw the once majestic tree now half its
original size, and dropped his bulbs.

I would swear on my Montblanc pen this Monte Carlo was the same vehicle that tailed me the previous night. My first thought: shake 'em. That's what you do when you're being followed. Everyone knows it. Not that anyone thinks it through. Losing a tail on a modern American street takes more skill than passing someone on a waterslide.

Skip it, I told myself. There were probably a thousand black Monte Carlo's registered in the greater Beau Fleuve area. I'm being paranoid. Except that I hadn't killed the location-loop-friend-finding gizmos on my phone. A good criminal would kill his signals. Loam seemed to be a good criminal — and perhaps thought enough of me to assume that I too might make a good criminal and eventually turn off my signals. So, if he wanted to keep an eye on me, he'd do it the old-fashioned way, with a tail.

Screw it. Spy away. Have fun watching me eat a hotdog, Loam. It's your three hours.

The parking ramp at the ballpark curled in on itself, nautilus style. I failed to see or hear anyone keeping up. As I made my way into the stadium, I began to relax a little.

Kai raised two beers when he saw me. I wouldn't mind warming the bench with him. We both spoke core English and I liked to talk. He spoke a colorful Northeastern trade variant of the tongue. I enjoyed hearing it. English is the one of the most expressive of the live languages. Used in conversation by people who have more than glancing knowledge, it can be entertainment in and of itself, though a fading form. With the slow death of English, I also foresee the loss of conversation as art. Every coffee house from Beau Fleuve to Los Angeles will go still. The music in jazz clubs will crescendo uncontrollably from lack of competition. People will begin to wonder why those front porches on those old houses were ever built.

English ain't easy. That's its prime incurable ailment. The secondary concern: Nobody needs to learn it. If you go to work and speak Market, and come home and speak Market, and then watch your favorite celebrity celeb in Market, what's the point of struggling to learn anything else? The world's complicated enough. I don't expect my favorite tongue to go into remission. It doesn't have much to live for. For most, it passed away long ago.

Professional interpreters learn English as a tool. A Rosetta Stone. It's key to understanding all of the off shoots. Sometimes women I'm trying to impress are amazed to hear that I'm proficient in thirty-four argots and conversant in about twenty more. Those aren't even great numbers for an interpreter. The trick is to learn the root language first. English, in America. Once you have that one planted in your head, it's a slight chore to learn the branches. Remember, *positive* is very bad if you're talking to doctor and very good if you're talking to a management consultant. It's juggling synonyms. If more people learned the root tongues in the first place, I'd be — all interpreters would be — selling pretzels from kiosks on street corners.

Cold beer, a footlong hotdog with mustard, onions, kraut, relish and sprouts, a game program in my phone and sitting five rows up from the field. Royal. The sun peeked over the bleachers like a three-year-old at bedtime, dragging out one last glimpse of what the grownups were up to.

Glaring blueish white lights, fans meandering, pointing at seat numbers, buying peanuts, and scolding children who cried for souvenirs. Kai slid his dog into his mouth, not yet used to his beard.

The teams marched out. We stood for the National Anthem. Everyone cheered at the end. Most, because the game would now start. Me, because they still belted the song out in English. Baseball is intelligent, careful, and hewn on years of tradition. Algorithms have not yet pruned the game beyond recognition. It's still played outside, subject to the whims of the weather, with bags and balls and pudgy gloves. No, they didn't have the ceramic bat when the Babe was playing. And no, lasers didn't call foul balls to the nearest micron for Honus Wagner, but if you brought Aaron or Mays forward in time, they wouldn't be so lost that they couldn't hit the hide out of the park.

Baseball is also a large portion of the population's second language. Whether fans speak Bio, Sec, or the Japanese versions of the same, when the ump thrusts his thumb in the air and says "He's OOUUUT!" everyone knows what he means and cheers or curses accordingly. The ball field is common ground. For some, it's the only ground they ever share.

"What's the word, Will?" Kai looked out at the field. "There a reason behind your new found weirdness?"

"I've had some weird things happen to me."

"That jam session with the cops?"

"That was just the start. It's become less believable since."

"Roll, baby, roll. You're so out there I've got to hear anything taking you deeper into the ozone." He took another chomp of his hotdog and slug of his beer.

"After working a murder investigation, a beautiful woman broke into my apartment just to talk and I think I'm being followed."

"Crushing." He looked at me and then turned his head at the crack of a bat. Long ball to center. Snagged. First out.

Kai's expression was a fit response if I'd said, "my bedroom's beige" or "I like ice cream." Did I have "Imagination

Wildy Out of Control" tattooed to my forehead? What did it take to impress this guy? I told him most of my story, leaving out names, even though he possessed the inductive powers to attach at least Arthur Loam to the tale. I didn't mention Loam being a murderer and maybe wanting to kill again. Some things are better left unsaid.

That should have been my motto. I should've had that tattooed, not to my head — I can't see that — maybe to my forearm. Or the back of my hand. Then I'd be reminded regularly. I'd know something like the back of my hand and it would matter.

"And I thought my life was trackless," Kai said. "You're off the road."

"Caroming towards a carom, I imagine."

"Sorry I tugged."

"No, it's good to talk to someone, out loud, in English."

"Know what you mean," Kai said. "English. That effluvial cornucopia of words. Like *sublate*." He gave me a dare.

"You're getting carried away." I answered. "Excogitate?"

"Now you're thinking. Time to masticate?"

"You've bitten off more than you can chew."

The crowd roared as another ball rocketed into right field. The fielder scrambled. The Bison on third ran for home.

"Run! Run!" the software engineers in front of us shouted. And everybody knew what they meant.

Kai picked the bar after the game. The Battery. His kind of place. The air conditioning had that too-hot-to-work attitude. The lighting hadn't shown up for work at all. The bar had the scent of seven hundred different colognes sizzling on moist skin. The Mother Thomas Quintet cooked jazz — undulating, coruscating, the kind I can stand, even enjoy, so long as I can talk over it.

My car struggled to find a parking space and Kai beat me to the bar. He'd settled into a lean, way back on both elbows, next to the Martini he'd ordered and I aimed to drink whether it was mine or not. He chuckled when I picked it up and sipped deep.

"You haven't met my new friend yet, have you," he said.

"If she's responsible for this beard, I'd like to."

"She's responsible for the tickets, actually. So be nice."

"I can only be me."

"They're winding tight, man." He nodded towards the band, tapping his fingers on his long-neck beer.

"They're playing real instruments. I'll give em that."

Jazz and baseball match nicely. American originals, both overcoming the world's language barriers. Baseball by teaching everyone a side lingo, jazz by abandoning verbiage altogether. Though part of me thinks the listener is getting less. When you crank old Public Enemy lyrics you're getting love, hate, grief and groping and grandstanding. Words. You're getting twice the bang for your buck.

Kai leaned in. "You are allowed to enjoy things without words, too."

"Just not as much."

"You're missing out on some wonderfully wordless activities."

"I'll take your word for it." I held my glass up. He met it with his bottle. I leaned back against the bar, panning the room. Heads and shoulders all moved in different ways at the same time. Little groups congealed and laughed, glued by whatever business they'd just escaped. Pairs huddled and grinned. Singles took refuge in that natural focal point the band offered. My eyes roved from the stage, over the swaying people, to the door. White heels, sleek legs, tight candy-striped suit. The woman's hair had fallen across what I presumed was her very pretty face. As she approached the bar, I quickly prepared my smoothest smile for—

Andrea Breen tucked her hair back into place as she finished strutting towards me. I sucked up some cocktail in a gasp. A massive cough seared the back of my throat. I would die trying to hold it.

"Hi, Perk." That luscious voice.

Through drowned eyes, I saw her snake around Kai and kiss him like they were in high school.

No. Unacceptable. This was not Kai's fabulous new other. Fabulous yes, but—

"Glarf." I made the noise out loud. Not that they noticed half inside each other's mouths.

After a sloppy parting they turned to me.

"Andrea, this is my pal, Will. Will, Andrea."

She held out her hand. I took it as one might a fresh grub.

"It's nice meeting with you," she said. "The reports have been bullish."

"I'm ... yes."

Kai gave her a squeeze. "This is Andrea's first time here."

"It must be." I winked at her. "I certainly would have remembered seeing you before." Ah, old lines. This one proved useful, me not being able to form an original thought just then.

I turned back over the bar to replace my empty Martini glass with something more fulfilling. The band played "Take Five," so I did. From the happy couple. I let them chitchat and tried to look completely enraptured by the music, lilting in five-quarter time.

Kai must have met her at work, through Loam. What a capital explanation. They simply met during a meeting. He helped her conjugate *subvert*. It's an adorable story.

Or, my mind spun, she'd been tasked by Loam to keep an eye on Kai. As interpreter, Kai knew a great deal about Loam's plans and plots. If Kai were going to leak to anyone it would be this sumptuous new companion. Leaks would flow back to Loam. Then, when I'd borrowed the Rigoletto's timeshare and came in to pinch interpret, he'd assigned her to me as well. All of which was easier than killing Paul Dombrowski.

"Hey, Will," Kai craned back to me, "keep her entertained for a second. I've got an urge to purge."

Andrea turned, red lips drawn to the left. I felt like an hors d'œuvres.

"How did you finish today, Will?"

"Even for the day, thank you." I played it suave. I would stay suave. Unswaying suaveity.

"This property is prime. I'd take a piece."

"You could call it the Blue Chip?"

She laughed and gently touched my forearm. "My report said you were a player."

"My report on you is in draft form."

"Good. And I value the discretion re Kai. A little inside information retains friends." She moved closer but turned her head out towards the band. "We should be friends."

"Like Kai and I are friends? Friends for three fiscals? The brand of friend that doesn't let the other into the red?"

We looked straight at each other, her dark eyes, simmering liqueur in the half-light of the jazz club. My eyes .... I had no idea.

"Sure." She looked back at the band. "Just like that."

A verbal pat on the head. A six-year-old explaining his theories on the Easter Bunny would have elicited more respect. I could think what I wanted to think, say what I wanted to say, none of it mattered.

"Hey." Kai took Andrea's hand as he stepped next to us. "Will chairin' this conference? Once he gets the floor...."

"No. We've cochaired. Your associate is very generous."

"That's what I reported. A genuine trustee, he is." They both looked at me and smiled.

There are words that pair so nicely they become common phrases. High and low. To and fro. Touch and go. People can be like that. Kai and Andrea weren't. They went together like claret and suds. Their whole concept bent wrong. Kai didn't know it, or care. Andrea did, per her job. I fit with them lock, stock, and peril. Time to go.

But I hesitated. When I left, they'd talk about me. Kai would relay to her everything I'd said at the ballpark. He might phrase it like a defense of my mood or character. She would take it as a report on my stability.

I'd said nothing and too much.

I talk too much. Professional life aside, there is no reason for me to go around spouting off about everything that happens to me just because I enjoy the vulgar display of vocabulary and the exercise of my jaw. I don't know why nobody ever told me that. Sure, it would have been like telling me not to breathe, but you can always say, "Don't breathe so much." Because, I assure you, if too much oxygen can be hazardous, too much talking can be even worse.

Could I be wrong? Could I afford not to be careful? I already succeeded in laying out for Kai the blanket of information I had patched together. Kai knew that I knew too much. He knew that I'd had extended conversations with the police and, worse, that I had produced an apercu on Loam. I had not turned out to be, what they call in business, a laydown: someone easily mollified; someone inconsequential; a person who responds to threats as sheets do to folding.

No. I was a man who peeks under the covers.

The band finished "It Had to Be You". The silence of the break gave me the chance to say goodbye with aplomb.

"I'm done. Beat, Kai." I stretched and tipped my head. "You two try to have some fun."

The heat, the humidity, the strain from trying to look cool, it all got to me. I needed to go home and turn off for a while. I mentioned this to the car and it started us on our way.

I would have preferred to turn invisible and stay in the club. Would Andrea start drilling for information right away or wait until later, when Kai had less blood in his head and more alcohol? Or did they not give a shit? Could I be wrapped so tightly into myself that I imagined they cared? What was that word? Solipsistic? Here sat William Kirst, center of the universe.

"Get over yourself," I said.

"Pardon," the car said back.

"Disregard."

My Saab eased me down Main Street, under the arc lamps and neon signs, past the donut shops and people roaming the night.

"Driver's window down twenty-five percent."

The sounds of the street were real and lively and unpredictable. Without trying, at the stoplight, I heard three different lingos. A cluster of engineers, seeking slurry. Three bankers wanting to deposit themselves somewhere decent. Two H-VAC guys roared about some other guy's chute. A faint smell of pretzels made me wonder about that interpreter that used to work for my firm, the one who got fired or sick of it all or both. I wondered if he liked his hotdog cart.

A black Monte Carlo pulled in four cars behind me. I stopped smelling pretzels and the ghosts of hotdogs past. My car's tiller slid through the track in the road; the car had its program. I couldn't speed up, couldn't slow down. The Saab would take me home. A trackless car, like the cops have, that's what I needed. Jerk up the tiller and jump curbs and skid around corners with life screaming out of my tires.

That couldn't happen. I did the next best thing.

"Joystick. Manual mode."

A rubber half-banana rose from the center console. I took it in my hand and hoped I remembered how to use it, not remembering the last time I tried. The mechanics test it every year for the annual inspection, but I never did. Every place I ever went was already programmed into my car. I never went any place new. Larry's, Rigoletto's, The Battery, even the police station sat in my car's memory. My life was 100 percent on file. Whoever followed me should have been able to meet me wherever I was going.

Three left turns would tell me if I was neurotic or being tailed. I pushed the grip for a hard left at the next corner. The Saab turned, tiller gliding through the deep groove in the road. No rubbing. Very smooth. It does come back to you. At the next intersection I waited for a break in traffic. The coupe rolled up directly behind me — big, black, American. I think it scared my little car. With the windows inky from the tinting and the glare of the streetlights, the Pope could've been following me, and I wouldn't know.

I turned left. Three cars fell in. The Monte Carlo turned to follow. My stomach clenched. Nobody programmed a route like this, a big circle. I had a tail. An honest-to-Hollywood tail.

"Auto, photograph rear," I said. "Repeat last. Repeat last." I didn't bother to look at the car's monitor. I tried for a quality image through quantity.

I turned left for a third time, and his eminence kept going straight. Maybe he panicked? Maybe he didn't want a confrontation? Yeah. I scared off one of Loam's hired thugs. That was an idea to get behind.

"Auto, home." I let go of the joystick and poked the car's media center. I brought up video the car's cameras had recorded for the last few minutes. I paused on a shot from the rear camera. The image on the main monitor didn't have enough light, but someone's headlights hit the Monte Carlo's front plate during a turn. I could read the license number without enhancing the image at all. I bumped the image to my phone and gave myself a mental pat on the back. I won that game.

Of course, I didn't know it would be a doubleheader.

Chapter 11

From "Tales without Interpreters"
The mechanic told the media developer that his car had
sustained frontend damage. The media developer blew
a big sigh of relief. Frontend. Ha. Superficial, cosmetic,
graphical crap. That was great. He'd been worried the
damage had been serious, backend stuff. He'd drive it
home. The mechanic protested vigorously. The media
developer ignored him for three fourths of a mile, right
until the passenger-side wheel popped off.

Once I'd lost my tail, and the adrenaline passed its peak,
I became much more interested in sleeping than anything
else. My Saab stopped obediently in my parking slot. As I
got out, I noticed someone in a dark suit standing outside my
apartment building's front doors.

I ventured as far as the end of my trunk when that sixth
sense we all have, the one that tells you when the person in
the car next to you is looking over, made me shoot a peek to
my left.

"Hi, Will." The voice sounded like wet stones in a sock.
It matched the rest of him quite nicely.

Why hadn't I seen him standing there when I pulled
in? Midforties, dressed in a navy, pinstriped suit that
failed to fool me — this guy went to business school
in an alley. His classmate kept watching from the front
door.

"Time for a conference," the man next to me said.

"How 'bout the morning? I'm more of a morning person."
Take gin and heat, and agitate. The cocktail let my mouth
function all on its own.

"Hey. You got options with this proposal. This doesn't have to be hostile." He spoke Business, more or less, but his elocution wasn't exactly boardroom quality.

"Meet with your boss and submit this — I deal with top dogs," I looked him up and down, "not their leavings."

"What you need is a crash course in employee relations, junior. And I'm gonna instruct." He sneered, clenched his fists and moved forward. Sometimes you can talk yourself into a fight even faster than out of one.

No time to get back in the car. Could I take him? The other representative from human resources started towards us, keeping himself between me and the front door of my apartment building. Could I take both? That was the gin asking. The real me knew the answer. Behind the real me stood a ten-foot chain link fence, which had much more appeal.

The pinstriped man reached for me, hand like a claw. I ducked back, spun, and jumped up onto the hood of my car. He moved quickly. He rounded the trunk and dove for an ankle tackle, but I pounced higher onto the mesh fence than I would've thought possible. His elbows bounced off the Saab's rubbery hood. He couldn't reach me over the car and would have to jump up on top himself.

I scrambled to the top of the fence like a rabid squirrel and flipped over, letting the wire prongs at the top take a couple pokes at me. The man looked at me through the fence in total disgust and then smiled.

My plunge to safety was interrupted as fence spikes skewered the back of my suit jacket, and held me in place, a goose in the butcher shop window.

The other guy charged up, saw my predicament and started to laugh. I didn't see the humor in it; this being one of my better, tailored khaki summer suits.

"How's it hangin', junior?" one said and the other laughed.

Ha ha. So funny I had to choke.

I tugged with one hand, but the jacket wouldn't give. Strong material. They shook the wire mesh, laughing. I flapped and banged about, a fish in a net. The undulations wriggled me more than the jacket. We all noticed. They stopped laughing. I planted my heels against the mesh, leaned out and pulled in my arms. I dropped like a newborn giraffe into the thick, dry bushes, chest first.

The crash caused so many kinds of pain it almost didn't hurt. The scrapes and pokes and impact were too much to process. Breathe. That became the single point of concentration. Breathe. The men in suits scaled the fence. I somersaulted out of the shrubbery, which I don't think looked too stupid. They rounded the top of the fence, taking more care than I had.

I bolted into the dark, not glancing back, but hearing crashes into bushes over the sound of my shoes slapping the pavement. I crossed the parking lot of an office building and rounded the corner. No place to hide. I only had a few meters on them. More fencing in front of me and to the right, so over I went.

My pursuers rammed the fence, almost grabbing my left foot. I flopped into some garbage on the other side and took off again. The chain-links clinked wildly behind me.

I ran into a back alley — by far the best place to be if you don't want anyone to interrupt as you have your teeth knocked out. I passed broken bricks, trash cans, and pieces of PVC tubing that were once probably very important to some machine. I had a vague understanding of the street I was headed for, but had more interest in the sounds of pounding feet behind me.

This was not one of the most inviting parts of downtown. Beau Fleuve's crime rate doesn't show up next to New York's or Miami's, but it's not a city of angels. In the middle of the night, I raced into the part of town that proved it.

The redbrick alley made the clapping of their footsteps louder and bigger, beyond two men, they sounded like a gang of gangsters with nothing better to do than run down some poor interpreter whose only crime was talking too much.

The alley debouched into a thin, quiet side street. I darted left on nothing but instinct. A grocer had closed for the night. Who could blame him. The cleaner, hat blocker, Ronda's Readings, all closed. My heart punched at my breastbone. My lungs heaved. I heard the scuffs of shoes on concrete, steadily growing. A couple of cars passed. No one had any interest in people running for their lives. You can watch posts of that any time you like.

It always thought this city had a bar on every corner, but there never seemed to be one — let alone a cop for God's sake — when you need one. I made a plan: obfuscation. I needed to call the cops while not offering a clear shot from the gats I knew these mugs kept in shoulder holsters under their jackets. I had to break into one of these places, and make them guess which one.

I zipped across the street, rummaging my soul for every ounce of speed I could muster, and still use, in my loafers.

Two buildings in from the corner, on the right side, was a boarded-up green structure, with a front door ajar. Lights seeped from the inside, along with thumping music. 'Mondo's' had been sprayed in orange across a pine plank in all caps and set inside what had probably been, at one time, the front window of a barber or bridal shop.

I barely made the turn towards the door without complete loss of balance and my last atoms of dignity. I hit the door running.

"Two dents, biter. And ice up." The bouncer wore black jeans, boots, and a chain of steel braided with glowing blue optic-fiber. It crossed his beer-keg chest from his left shoulder down to a single belt loop on his right hip and then up his back. Sunglasses helped disguise his true age, though I thought it might be somewhere just under my own. He had a merchant phone in his fist, and I don't think he ever had trouble keeping it there.

The ruckus of my entrance stopped no one's smoking, drinking, fondling, staring into nothingness, or playing pool. The room had no lighting. My — anyone's — ability to see came courtesy of a dull green glow of the billiards area, the harsh beckoning of the beverage dispenser and the various luminous accessories the kids wore. A planetarium without all that confusing science.

Details became whispers in the sound and darkness. Lots of denim and battered leather, rips and drawstrings, the sounds of artificial jazz and scents of sugar, tea and pot. A Coke machine stood in the back next to two coolers that claimed to have drinks not so soft. The furniture all had a pushed-to-the-curb look, everything worn past salvation and refusing to match. This wasn't a club, so much as a kind of rec-room or the basement of parents way, way out of town. Half this crowd looked young enough to still live at home, the other half looked like they'd been kicked out.

"I said two dents!" The bouncer held up two fingers, either illustrating the amount of money he needed from me or getting ready to poke my eyes in. Dents, short for Presidents, who decorated most American currency. I pulled out my phone and transferred the money to his.

"What's your hunt?" Now that he had my money, he got around to asking the obvious. I certainly didn't look like a regular and from the volume of my breathing, he knew I hadn't walked here. He would toss me if I couldn't prove I wasn't a cop or parole officer or creep.

Standing there, gasping for air, bleeding from skinny scratches across my cheeks on forehead, in khaki pants and a dressy shirt, I didn't know what this guy would swallow. A couple of kids watched to see if the bouncer would lift me off the ground by my pant waist and chuck me hay-bale style.

"I'm a missionman, Tank," I said, "but my mission sawed. My pack broke." The bouncer kept at me with a stern, disbelieving face. I looked around a bit, like I didn't care what the Hell he thought.

"You a missionman?" He sneered.

"Your ears on? Way. Fillin' some holders. These nats show. Blades, pops, we all broke."

"You ditched here?" He reached for me, not wanting any trouble tracked in. Two other guys with nothing better to do walked over. They stood ready to help the bouncer bounce me, like he needed any assistance.

"Hey! Ice!" I backed up and raised my open hands in what I hoped read as a guested of controlled placation "Need to get off the ment for a tick — de-harsh, track?"

I continued to back up. The boys faded away and the bouncer shrugged to let me past.

Making my way to the back of the room, trying to hide my desperate need for oxygen, I counted about twenty-five young people. Quite a few younger than I'd initially thought, probably midteens. I didn't know how much time I had before Loam's men wandered in, so I looked for a nook to hide in or back door to jet through and fingered my pocket for my phone.

A girl in cut-offs and a black cross-over shirt-wrap-thing leaned back against the Coke machine, one leg planted on plastic crate, showing off the radiant, deep purple optic-fiber that snaked from under her shorts down into her ankle boot. She watched me through dark, hacked bangs, obviously curious about so fresh a face in her old hangout.

"You a tag?" Her full, windy voice got up and over the music. It sailed on the verge of nasty. I think she looked at me, but couldn't say for sure though the hanging hair. Pity. Her interest in me made her interesting.

"No. Not a tag." I waved my phone in front of the Coke machine, forcing myself to be aloof.

"You ain't no sniffer," she said.

"Nope." A soda can tumbled out of the machine.

"Sooooo...." She waited.

"Sooooo, I'm a runner. Cranked too many UV's, had to get off the beach. Track?" I drew in a sip of my beverage and hoped my phrase hadn't sounded out of date. Did kids still talk about ultraviolet light as if it were heat? Did crank remain in fashion?

"You too nat to be a missionman," the girl stated.

She thought I was too well dressed to run messages. I couldn't change what I wore, so I'd have to amp up my attitude.

"You balled it all, huh? Know every tag and sniff and mission on the cement?" I looked around the room. "You not balled me."

I leaned back on the machine. The hard-guy act got easier with every syllable. Even a little fun. Doing this every night would put me in therapy, but for the moment I enjoyed myself.

Another kid came over, holding a cue-stick. He couldn't have been more than nineteen, dressed in the dingy uniform of the club, blond hair straight to his shoulders, with a single glowing, red fiber woven in, dropping down the right side. He checked me out from head to toe and then looked at the girl next to me.

"Who's the biter?" he asked her.

"Q him. I don't know." She folded her arms across her chest.

"Got a fill, biter?"

"Will."

"When?"

"Always."

"Always what?"

"Always Will."

"Will, like William." The girl lost her patience.

"Oh," the boy said.

"Your poke, Roger." A black-haired youth on the edge of the pool area shouted over, which took some athletic lungs.

Roger sauntered back to the game, giving the cue-stick a flick to make sure the cable that came out of the back, and into the ceiling, wasn't going to impede his next shot.

"Fill's Claire." The girl watched Roger size up the position of the balls of light hovering in green space.

I loved that word, *fill*, as in what you use to fill in blanks, prompts, or boxes. It's not necessarily your name.

"Hi, Claire," I said back.

Roger had solids and three balls remaining before he could try for the eight. The opponent had five stripes. His stance suggested he'd try to put the bright, blue two-ball in the far, upper right pocket. The cue-ball floated three feet off the ground and a foot in front of him, the two-ball held almost midfield, so he had to squat down for the shot.

The cue-ball floated three feet off the ground and a foot in front of Rodger. He had just one remaining before he could try for the eight. Unfortunately, the two balls kissed near the far, upper right pocket. A tight little pair. Like some of the kids here.

They spoke in pidgins to one another. Nouns from one dialect, verbs from the other. Halfway between languages to half understand each other. It happened in schools all the time, friends trying to talk, trying to connect. Those tight little pidgins never reformed into a broad, common tongue. There were too many languages to smash back together. A Med and a Tech could probably create their own, fully formed hybrid language, but it wouldn't take the accountants into account. Or the artists or actuaries or all the many and various vocations. It would also take time. Time hates language. Erosion, contamination, ambiguation. You can't hit one ball into other balls until they all rerack.

"Your night must have really sawed to ditch in this playground."

"Yep. Must lay in a tic fore the nats track in. They ain't up to givin' off."

"No nats pound in here. No nats ball the box." She half snickered, finding some humor in the realization that most people, even those walking by every day, never noticed this place. It was an invisible storehouse for the idle youth. A depository for those too young to hit the bars and begin legal alcohol dependency, and too old and social to stay at home and sit with their parents watching disparate posts on disparate screens. They didn't have the money for clubs or the transport to anywhere else. They had this hovel. Nobody saw it because nobody cared.

Claire's words betrayed intelligence. Enough to make me wonder if she'd end up dead from an overdose, or stray bullet, or actually make it through school and show others that she had savvy beyond her appearance. The street jargon would hold her back. The minute a guidance counselor or college admissions officer heard a word of this street lingo, she'd be labeled as prostitute or soon-to-be-prostitute. She'd have to lose the tongue if she wanted to go anywhere in life.

Roger took a skillful stroke at the cue ball. Compressed air shot down the cable on the back of the stick and hit a valve inside to make it feel like he had struck a real, Belgian ivory orb. The cue bounced off his last ball with what I imagined might have been a click — the music was too loud — sending it into the far, upper right pocket. The blue ball disappeared. He lined up his next play.

"You see a lot," I said to Claire.

"I look," she returned.

"You know the word **clever**?"

"Sharp. Like a cleaver."

"Why you doing time in this box?"

"I can prompt you for the same ask."

That made me smile. "You could mark." I looked at her. "If you wanted."

Her head tilted — curiosity fighting mistrust. I don't think she had a response ready for compliments involving her brain.

Through the glimmer of the pool-field I could see the faux businessmen open the door. Nattily dressed, the kids would say. Nat for short. The bouncer put out his hand and then put it down. He lost his tyrant stance, slumping around the neck and shoulders.

The older suit walked in. The music pounded. As he came further into the room, I could see what made the previous ruler abdicate. A matte-black pistol pressed against the bouncer's left temple by the younger of my pursuers.

I hadn't thought far enough ahead. I'd let my mind rest, waver, the girl, the jazz, frolicking lights in the billiard field. I didn't want any of these kids shot at just because I never shut up. Why'd the gangsters have to pull a gun? Really? Could I possibly warrant that? I hadn't dropped my oath. Never. I didn't deserve this.

I dropped the soda can as I walked forward, stopping dead center of the translucent pool cube. No one missed the overdressed, overaged man in the human aquarium. Everyone stopped flirting, drinking, dragging, pretending they'd already seen it all at seventeen.

The suit sneered and used his thumb for a quick motion in the direction of the door. I smiled, made the universal hand sign for a pistol, put it to my head and then lowered it. He shook his head and reached inside his jacket. His hand emerged with a pistol. I wished I knew what kind, then chided myself for wasting brain power again. It was big enough, I knew that much. This gat had the caliber to kill me and maybe the poor bastard behind me.

The music pumped and sprang.

The man walked towards me, arm out straight, gun level with my forehead. I thought about that look on Paul Dombrowski's face as they slid him into the coroner's van and wondered if mine looked the same right now. The gun got bigger. I saw the index finger tightening around the trigger. Stupid me. Why not shoot me right here? Who'd say a word?

Two slender arms entwined around my left one. Claire put herself right up against my left side and stood there, staring the gunman down through her bangs.

The man in the suit changed expressions. Deadly grin gone. He glanced right and left. The cocky curl of his lip fluttered. He bared his teeth at me, like he wanted to lunge and bite. He pointed his gun up in the air and rolled his fingers along the grip.

I moved my head slightly to get a read on the room, then I couldn't stop looking.

Just about every kid in the place had a gun pointed at my two pursuers. Big pistols, little pistols, black, brown, nickel. One tyke, girlfriend still on his lap, held a chubby multibarreled thing I would've thought more appropriate for a ship deck mount. Exciting, relieving and disturbing. They didn't know me, but they weren't going to let Claire get plugged.

The men backed out, guns in the air. My breathing resumed. I kissed Claire on the top of her head. The child-queen had rescued the bedraggled knave. Without uttering a word.

She led me through a hole in the back of the clubhouse that attached it to an unlit, closed-for-the-night parking garage. She pointed deep into the place. I didn't know what to say. I smiled and left.

I walked in the direction Claire had indicated, not feeling like I had one — a direction that is — through the garage and onto a street supporting a number of warehouses. The location was only slightly less dangerous than the one I'd left, but I could at least hear traffic. Home and work were no longer options. A hotel sounded too much like the choice of a fugitive and I wasn't ready to stick myself with that label.

I took out my phone. My hand shook so bad I had to use both to call a cab.

Chapter 12

From "Tales without Interpreters"
The broker was notoriously cheap, but he wanted in on the
deal. He asked his wife, an English teacher, to look over
the contract. "First," she explained, "the capitalization is
all wrong." He nodded and decided right there to step back
from the investment. His wife circled the 'S' in summer.
He lost out on millions.

Larry opened the door, eyes mostly shut and crusty. He wore
blue silk boxers Ann must have bought him.

"Ping." He shuffled away, not looking back.

"Thanks. Really," I whispered.

He disappeared into a dark kitchen. I followed, thinking
a glass of water might be smart.

"Query total spike, Will?" Larry finally woke up enough
to ask.

"PM run bugged." I found a glass. "Two viruses at my
rack, programmed to initialize."

"If."

"Then. I purged from the site. Lined at my top rate."

"End run here?"

"Off. First downloaded to a club-site cross-stacked with
chips. Viruses traced and brought some serious mechanical-
energy hardware online. Projectile."

"Off!" He was horrified and fascinated at the same time.

"On. Pre total mega-crash, the viruses aborted their
program." Larry gapped at me waiting to hear what happened
next.

"The chips brought their hardware online. Total. Mega,
micro, high-rate, a fried full rack of projectiles."

"Surge, man."

"Total."

Saying it out loud didn't make the story sound all that believable, really. Slouching in the oak dinette chair, bleeding from my hands and face, in a half-tattered shirt, my tale had an acceptable level of credibility. Besides, as I've said before, Larry always thought my life to be seven times more interesting than it was, which was prescient. Hour by hour my life got closer and closer to his version of my truth.

"Inquest into the consul, boys." Ann glided in, looking just as put together in her shiny, silk wrap as she did all day in proper clothes. Her voice didn't possess the usual warm, welcome tone. She was annoyed until she saw me. Then the maternal, medical instincts raced ahead of the anger. She glanced at the scrapes across my hands, head, and face and sped off into another room.

"Goto medbag," Larry explained.

She came back before I finished my next sip of water.

"May I inquest the pathology of your lacerations?" She dropped her first aid kit — a nylon bag that was more *Mom* than *medical professional* — onto a nearby chair.

"Altercation," I answered as she unfolded a flap that had several vials and boxes strapped to it. "Metallic protrusions to hands and organic lacerations to face."

"How long ago?"

"Two hours."

"Negative treatment? Idiot. Infection, tetanus. Possible trauma to the head?" She may have been joking about that last bit. I couldn't be sure. How would I know?

She cleaned my wounds in the most painful way possible. All kinds of swabbing and searing pain. I could not fathom how something so awful could be good for me. I guess if I were a germ, I wouldn't have stuck around. I didn't want to stick around.

"Your visitation is benign," Ann said. "You would have allowed the lacerations to fester."

She had me there. I wouldn't have given them a thought until they were all red and suppurating. She dressed the wounds in pure white gauze. That alone made me feel better.

People really shouldn't go around leaking fluids. Or without others to help them, though that latter part is not always easy.

"Overnight stay?" she asked. Or maybe told me. I looked at Larry.

"Command." He shrugged.

"I'll get a gown and linen." And she hopped off again.

After fleeing the backend of Mondo's club for kids, my first thought had been to race home. Not my apartment. My old home. My parents only lived twenty minutes from where I had been. I couldn't make the call. Any call to retired people after ten at night means someone's dead or dying. Pops would've been fine seeing me all cut up and bruised. The mother — she would've quivered and cried and ended up sick for the next week. I didn't want to bring my troubles back to them.

Infecting Larry and Ann didn't bother me as much. They were young and resistant and there they were, all pillows and blankets, tourniquets and towels.

Ann dropped off a load of clean laundry, turned out the lights, and vanished without a sound.

In a fetal position on the sofa in the family room — halfway to being a burrito in all of Ann's fresh linen — so exhausted I would have curled up in a coffin — my mind refused to switch over to dreaming. Would those guys really have shot me dead? Could Andrea have upped the command from *surveil* to *silence* — the transitive verb — after I left The Battery? Seemed too quick. Too compressed. The black car. The muscle already at my apartment. I felt like I'd started watching my show at episode three or four, which was impossible, me being the star and all. Not, obviously, the writer. Oh, to author one's own story. Control. Power. Happy endings. Comfortable as I was, I would've written a much better scene for myself. Swanky apartment. A lovely woman opens the door just enough to see one smokey eye. Andrea Breen. No.

I started thinking about Kai Farino. I'd known him for three years. It's a long time to hold your breath, but it ain't much for getting to know a guy. He'd had been at Burgess and Huxely the day I started. We harmonized immediately.

"You're melliferous for an interpreter," he'd said as I strolled the halls like a country boy on his first trip into the big city.

"Don't start, honey," I'd replied without stopping. He'd roared. He'd found a new playmate. I became his favorite partner in office gossip, gripes about the clients who could barely speak their own professional tongues and upper management who spent more time at lunch than they did facilitating. Fresh out of college, I'd never actually been an agency interpreter. Kai covered the curricula they don't offer in school:

(1) If you don't know a word, make one up and look at your clients like they're savages for not knowing it themselves. A client's confidence in the interpreter ranks first, far above diplomacy and truth.

(2) Interpreters control the speed and tone of every meeting. Don't be afraid to exercise it. If they're too slow, speed it up. If a client's an asshole, make sure everyone knows it but him. If they want to argue and you don't, just shut up and they can't keep going.

Most important: (3) The only true reason to do this for a living is to be able to talk to lots of potential romantic partners. It's not the fringe benefit, it's the point. If you don't take advantage of this gift, it is a sin to Shelley, Keats, and Miller.

Kai's motivations had always been straightforward and easy to identify. Loam would have figured Kai out in seconds and crafted the right way to manipulate his thirsts. Straight, white male, single, aged thirty-one, watches the office assistant's ass like a hummingbird circling a fresh gardenia.

I am out of my league, I thought to myself. How trite and yet, how appropriate. I'm sitting there at the ball game, gabbing away like I'm some kind of player. *Playa'* they say in my favorite songs.

A big shot,
'til he gets shot,
with a gat,
through the nat—
ty suit.

Bloodstains don't come out
Not with Shout....

I could rap. Totally, I could. Keeping it real would be the tough part. I get one gun pointed at my head and I'm hardcore no more. Mushcore. That would be my street name. How did those guys do it? Running the streets with their AKs and Mac 10s — dodging the police and rival gangs, and still managing to put down some rhymes. It must have been amazing back then.

Day one, yo, growing up in the ghetto
Now I'm a weed fiend jetting to Palmetto

Sure, Raekwon and the Wu-Tang Clan glamorized their pasts, but they professed the gruesome parts. They also survived. Maybe it wasn't all that bad. Or, maybe they were interpreting. Using some of Kai's rules. Were all the cops dumb. Were girls all over them all night long. Did *Ghostface carry a black nine*? A nine-millimeter pistol, as in what could have been pointed at my head. My head that I couldn't put right. I'd been smart enough to survive. To make it here, to this couch. Then the smarts ran out. Nothing to focus on except my recent memories of the fact that I'd almost died. Me. An interpreter. A piece of office furniture. Usually no one shoots the furniture.

I wish Ol' Dirty Bastard had put out one God damned song about counting sheep. Just one.

Chapter 13

From "Tales without Interpreters"
The decision had been hard for the corporal. He needed
to get back to the family business, but he loved the army.
He knew his commanding officer was anxious to know, so
the moment he made up his mind he texted him: "I have
decided to resign." The warrant officer texted back: "I am
sorry to hear that." The corporal became indignant. He
thought the warrant officer wanted him in the squad, that
he wanted him to sign on for another tour. Screw it, he
thought, and texted: "Okay, then. I've decided instead to
resign."

Something had crawled up my nose. Cold and rubbery, it
didn't feel like anything that might have ridden down from a
nostril, nor would make it much farther upwards. Curiosity
and concern broke through the haze of my slumber.

"He he he." Muffled giggling circled my head.

I mushed my lips around and squinted into the
morning light. Where was I? Some woman's bungalow? A
pool house because Isla and I were too drained to make it
back up to the main house? A tweed couch, not quite long
enough for my legs to uncramp. What was stuck up my
nose?

My eyes were reluctant to let in the wide-angle laser
these people apparently kept focused on the back window
of their home. I had to force one eyelid, then the other. I
remained on my back, wrapped in a blanket, covered with
three-inch-high Martians and spacemen. I pulled a ripe,
green one from my right nostril and listened to the sound of
light feet dashing around the corner, into the kitchen.

I lay at Larry's, in the family room, befuddled and dumb. This is why I don't stay over at a woman's place after a night of frolicking. Yep. That's the reason. I hate being dumb. What was stuck up my nose?

The sun blasted through the window and over the tiny head of the Major Astro action figure posturing on my chest. My neck told me someone had put a Phillips-head screwdriver in the freezer for a night, removed it, and stuck it up into the base of my skull. I made none of the noises I wanted to spout.

The Martian from my nose was of the fully- poseable, deep green variety, complete with helmet and ion blaster and other gold and black Martian gear. Lawrence Jr. giggled from his vantage point around the corner. Toys spilled as I sat up wondering how long I had been the child's unwitting diorama.

"Lawrence," my voice had that rumbling, early morning sound, "get me some coffee."

"Cannot prep coffee." Lawrence's high, bodiless voice came from behind me.

"You're very smart. I'm certain you can perform the procedure."

"No hot hardware. Mom's orders."

My eyes caught a bathrobe Ann had laid over the back of the couch, so I decided to get up and make the coffee myself.

In the kitchen, Lawrence leaned up against the refrigerator, holding a red and silver, plastic jump-jet, ready to strafe evil aliens or oatmeal or whatever he didn't care for this morning.

"Good morning." I opened a random cabinet.

"Query — you're inserted into my rack?" Lawrence looked up at me, only half interested.

"I heard the coffee here was strong and responsive."

"Oh." That was good enough for him.

Six years old, shiny black hair like his mom's and dry humor from his father. I'm sure I would shudder if I learned his IQ. His tight red pajamas looked like a Major Astro space suit.

"Query you're not loaded to schoolsite?" I found the beans.

"Summer."

"Summer schoolsite?"

"Felt wrong."

"Oh." I poured the beans in the chopper and started the awful, but necessary, noise. When it stopped, I took a deep breath near the surface of the course powder and then dumped it into the coffee maker.

Talking to Lawrence could be challenging due to the fluidity of his code-switching. He jumped back and forth between Cyber and Medic with ease — and no warning. I had to pick one or the other. Some parents feel that it impedes a child's learning velocity to speak more than one language in a household and they've got millions of dollars in studies to prove it. What the studies kept forgetting to mention was that while the initial language learning process was slowed, the child's overall perceptiveness and social intelligence skyrocketed.

I think a bilingual upbringing is the best thing for them. The more words they know, the better off they are. Not that anything ever slowed Lawrence anyway.

We returned to the family room. As I sipped my java, I watched the kid play with his Major Astro Moonbase. Not having been around toys for a while, I found the complexity and detail enthralling. Larry had mentioned this playset to me around Christmas, before Santa brought it down the Crep chimney, but I hadn't actually seen it in person.

The action-figures were made of some conductive, malleable plastic. The bas-relief Moonbase unfolded into a gray square the size of a card table, with concealed ley lines of super-conductive material. The point was to place vehicles and figures on the spots or lines of super-conductive stuff. Then you used your phone to program in all sorts of actions and speeds. When you were done, you hit [RUN] and the whole playset came to life. Your very own live, stop-action movie.

My Major Astro figures never did that. Back in my day they just talked and shot micro-laser beams that parents' action committees claimed would blind a generation.

Slurping my hot coffee, watching the boy meticulously place Martians on plastic ridges and members of the Earth

Defense Force in six-wheeled rovers, I felt happy for the space program. The billions of dollars in high-tech material's research certainly made for happy little boys.

"Program astronaut run on log?" I asked the back of Lawrence's head.

"If/or. Uncertain prognosis." He carefully stood Major Astro next to Cynthia, the plucky scientist who always came up with the nifty invention that Astro used to save the planet a couple minutes before the end of each episode.

"Scrolling forward to schoolsite?"

"Nope."

"Query?"

"School's a surge."

"Lawrence." I tried to fake parental indignation. "Not true."

"Sorry. Valid. Schoolsite is malignant." He started to depress the small, colorful buttons under the roof of the main building on the Moon. You could tell it was the most important structure on the Moon because it also held the wall plug and carrying handle.

"Your satellites will LAN? That's meg?"

"Nope. Satellites process schoolsite as meg. They're surges too."

He didn't like that his friends liked school. I couldn't blame him for not looking forward to it. I had, but I'd been weird. I wanted to hear as many tongues as I could. Not everyone shared my proclivity and even if they did, language diversity declined with every generation.

Larry and Ann had chosen to settle in a community of predominately information technology people. Because Ann worked as a medical imagist, she spoke fluent Cyber and Medic — as well as one or two other cants. It had been a logical choice to live here. The children of cyber-professionals tend to be much more attuned to the new education system. Which only makes sense. If you like your teacher, you'll like school. If your teacher's a computer, well, you better like computers. It seemed that was true of Lawrence's classmates.

Lawrence gave me the impression that he had little fondness for learning math, history, and reading from a screen while wearing communal headphones. I didn't think school computers were necessarily *malignant*, still, I could sympathize. Being brought up in an IT community and going to a computer-filled school put you in a track. The silicon brick road. Among the things I am absolutely not is a psychologist, but it seemed to me that Lawrence's dislike of school might stem from his dislike of the path he had been put on.

That is a lot to pull out of a six-year-old saying school was a surge. Unless I was projecting. That always helps.

There are issues with the school system that Lawrence may have sensed already. As it would be impossible for a public-school teacher to speak all of the argots of the diverse students, they rely on computer translation. A voxbox is so impersonal and unresponsive I'm amazed that kids learn anything. Especially about themselves. Sitting at their cruddy little monitors, being force-fed lessons, and then spitting back answers in whatever tongue they speak at home doesn't seem like the best environment for a child. Children can do anything. When they start growing, they should be able to go in any direction they want, without any strings or posts to keep them on a certain angle. They should be planted in basics, watered from the Pierian Spring, and let to reach for the sun or the moon or whatever catches their starry eyes. This hydroponics approach to education — sticking a kid in a tube and labeling them with a career before they knew their own name always bothered me. It's all too preordained. If you speak Chemo around the house and then make a kid learn how to add, subtract, and provide through Chemo, what are the odds they're going to become an auditor or artist?

Lawrence placed three Martians on a smooth path encircling the lunar surface. He gently bent their tentacles and attached the blaster-rifles. Two spacemen sat in their heavily armed rover, their determined sneers easily seen through the blue-tinted, clear windshield. Lawrence moved their hands to the vehicle controls. He poked another order into the control building.

"Administer coffee, Will?" Ann's voice came out from the kitchen.

"Coffee positive, Ann. And good morning."

"Nearly good afternoon," she sang back. I could hear her smiling.

The house said, "Mr. Jennings is at the front door," in an exaggerated British accent. Ann bounded out of the kitchen, attempting to insert a gold-loop earring.

"Lawrence, Mr. Jennings is on site. Go scrub and dress." She opened the door.

"Hi, Mrs. Crep."

"Hi, Keith," she said to the young man entering her home, still tilting her head and finishing with her ear.

I glanced over at the guy. Tall, decent looking, though the brim of the hat seemed too large. Kids. He carried a small, burlap purse.

"Enter. Lawrence is prepping." Ann dashed away.

I looked down at Lawrence, who was not prepping. He put Major Astro on the roof of the headquarters. In his pajamas, he looked like a six-year-old Astro furiously trying to pull off an elaborate scheme in the last seven minutes of his show. His imagination rocketing off, exploring distant worlds, battling aliens, and soliciting the help of his tiny friends. How long would it last? I thought. How long before he forgot the words *Wormjet* or *Technoroid, Plot* or *Characterization*?

"Goodbye," Ann said and slid through the front door. Keith introduced himself and set his purse down. I would have been more congenial, but Lawrence started his program. The towers lit. Lasers blasted. Gray plastic rumbled. Major Astro turned and waved. Cynthia looked at a gizmo she held. The Martians raised their weapons. The rover started towards the green monsters. It stopped, backed up, then raced through them, bouncing the little creatures all over the pocked terrain.

Lawrence laughed as the truck continued to roll on its way, over the bumps and through the turns. The lights and sounds, continuing to blare and glare.

Fascinated by all the movement, I dropped to my stomach. The playset had come alive. It continued its performance until young Mr. Jennings mentioned that Lawrence should be dressed. He may have wanted to say the same thing about me, but lacked the authority.

"Hi, Keith. I am Will." I rolled over and sat up, offering my hand.

"Hi." He helped me up instead of shaking it. It made me feel old. His eyes lingered too long at certain parts of my face, reminding me that I appeared to have lost a fight with a bobcat. Other people's faces are unforgiving mirrors. I looked at my bandaged hands, they were damp from the perspiration. I ran my fingers over the scrapes on my forehead — one had missed my right eye by a lash. A pair of bruises on my right arm showed up well against the four crisscrossed lacerations.

"You should see the other bush," I said.

Keith forced a smile. I must have seemed like exactly the kind of guy he was being paid to keep out of the house.

"You up?" Keith kneeled next to Lawrence.

"On," he replied. "Query today's program."

"Fun, games, and activities, little bot. Fun, games and activities."

On the coffee table in front of me, amidst the oxygen tanks and spare surface-to-air missiles, I found my personal effects. Ann planned to burn my blood-garbage-mud-stained clothing, so she'd emptied my pockets onto the table. The tip of my phone flickered. I fanned out the screen to see I had three messages: my boss, Victoria; Officer Bremburg; and one from a number I didn't recognize. Whoever left message number three had a ridiculously unlisted account. I walked into the dining room.

Victoria had left a commatic message. In three words she was able to convey commination, command, and concern. Such economy. I called her back, saying I felt ill. Which I did, in many new ways. It took me close to forty words. Such excess.

Bremburg's message requested I return his call. To solve for the unknown, I had no choice but to call the number I failed to recognize. After two rings, I heard, "Mr. Kirst?"

"Who is this?"

"Andrea Breen. We need a meeting."

"Can't see the upside. I met with some of your associates last night and didn't exactly turn a profit. Nearly a total loss."

"They were not associates of mine."

"Loam's."

"No. They were not under Mr. Loam's employ, either."

"I don't … They weren't public sector authorities."

"We need a meeting."

"Is there a third party in this venture?"

"A drink. My place."

"I'll get back to you."

I pushed 'end'. I needed time to roll that exchange around in my head. Not Loam's boys? They were waiting for me. They weren't street people. Who else wanted me really, really quiet?

Maybe I had an answer. I sent Larry the photos on my phone. Then switched to voice.

"Ping," Larry answered.

"I lined you a set of graphics."

"Received. Junk. Stick to translating."

"Query, resolve the license plate number of the car?"

"Too black … oh. Affirmed."

"Query a data set?"

"Run the plate? Crash yourself." Larry lowered his voice. "Illegal procedure."

"Overwrite," I returned. "You are prime. The law's just one more firewall to you, and a pathetic one at that."

"Tracing is traceable."

"One number. Not a series."

"You are developing a pattern," Larry said. "An extra-legal pattern."

"Ha," came out of my mouth. A genuine, surprising, one-note laugh. "You've only seen the frontend."

"Not returning."

"Query?"

"Bug," Larry shouted in a whisper. "Bug me. Not returning. No data set. No record."

"It's a New York State plate?"

"This is charred. Seriously. Query the routine you've wrapped me into?"

"Unknown," I said without moving my lips.

"Meat meet later," Larry said.

"Out." We both disconnected.

Larry could not derive any information on the license plate. Scary, I guess. Maybe. My tolerance for such things had been growing lately. It would take something stronger to get me going. Two calls down. Perhaps another hit off the phone would start the heart racing. Time to call the cops.

"Hello, Officer Bremburg? This is William Kirst, you know, the mouthpiece?"

"Yeah."

"I'd like to report—"

"I'll interview at the scene the vehicle was last reported? Over?"

"I'm not—"

"The Gonzales case remains open, so this will wait until nineteen-hundred hours. Do you copy?"

Gonzales? I said to myself. That car theft I worked six months ago? My part had wrapped up before summer, had nothing to do with Bremburg — a homicide detective. He spoke nonsense. Intentionally.

Context is half of interpreting. Idioms and similes are the Scylla and Charybdis of any conversation. Try to navigate without decent situational awareness and they will suck you down or bite your head off. The cop had gone Ulysses on me — Joycean, not Homeric — leaving me with no context at all. I had no choice but to go along.

"I'll be there."

Click.

That exchange made me feel much better. Cops always speak in code to set up meetings after hours, at a park, far from the station house. Yeah. This would all go down like boiling tequila.

Chapter 14

From "Tales without Interpreters"
As the news post editor awaited his order, the deli owner
asked him why he had not posted the op-ed he'd written.
"Your copy isn't original," the editor replied.
"Of course not," the deli owner said. "Who's is?"
"Everyone's," the editor said. "Your copy's got to be fresh."
"I just made it yesterday."
"No, like brand new."
"What? You think I took this op-ed off a shelf?"
"It's just … I'd read it before."
"Before I made it? That's some trick. If you can do tricks
like that why you wasting your hours posting news?"
The editor shook his head. "Some days, I don't know."

I sat on the couch, wearing my best friend's wife's bathrobe.
The shower plumped me from wilting to upright, though
not to full bloom. That would have taken a variety of Mira-
cle-Gro I didn't want to ingest this close to noon. That was
not the garden path. If I had one strength it was putting off
cocktails until five o'clock, give or take a wedding, holiday
or other family function. Knowing one's strengths and weak-
nesses is crucial for success in everything from tennis to
interpreting. When you work for a general interpreting firm
you soon realize how much better your life can be if you
stick to facilitating in tongues you're good at and avoid the
ones with which you struggle. And it is not always a matter
of fluency. I could produce a perfect score on an agricultural
dialect exam. When it comes to using the argot, working
an actual meeting, I am trudging through slop. Every little
clause and phrase drags on me. I'm never, as they say in my

business, ahead of the heard. I know this, my boss knows this, and I don't do farm stuff. Everyone is better off.

My job in jeopardy, confounding phone calls, attacks on my person — it was time to play my strengths. Yes. The things I do best ... there are several. There are two. First, I would not have a drink before five. Second, my even greater strength: wasting time.

Here's another thing about interpreting that they don't teach you in school. There is a significant amount of downtime. It comes in small parcels that makes it tough to use. If you're booked for a sixty-minute meeting, there might be ten minutes of settling in before you have any words to hash. It might break up ten minutes early, because you're amazing and facilitated the hell out of that confab. That's twenty minutes every hour with you and your phone and the tacit command that you sit quietly, ears open. I usually fan my phone and read the news, the mail, baseball crap, check out new cars to see how they compare to my beloved Saab, restaurant and bar reviews, one of the industry journals like *Tales Without Interpreters* or *Hoe of Babylon*, then, on long days, where I've been left alone in a corner for what's adding up to a hundred and twenty minutes, I go where the world takes me. Where's my sister? Over the Atlantic? What's she carting, Wheat? What's the price of wheat? Where's the wheat going? Sheffield? What do they do with wheat in Sheffield....

I sat on the edge of the couch and tried to focus.

Victoria's call. Nothing could be done about work right now.

Bremburg's call. I'd get to that later, whether I wanted to or not.

Andrea Breen. She claimed that she didn't know last night's assailants, that the men who had chased me around my neighborhood were not hired by her employer. I had no reason to believe her. Logic gave me doubts, though. Her word choice, the strained up-octave climb in her voice, the uselessness of the whole assertion. She should want me to fear the methods Loam might deploy to keep me in line, not discredit them.

The Creps had a living room sandbox on the end-table next to the couch. I activated the big monitors on the wall across from me and brought up a city map centered on my apartment building. I drew my escape route as best I could remember, from the parking lot to Mondo's. I circled the places along the way that may have had cameras. Video feeds from last night could be interesting. They could also require a court order. Unless I were ... something I'm not.

I thought about scooting into town and ferreting for video in person. Face to face is almost always better. Almost. This might be one of those cases when people not sizing me up was a plus. I'd have to forfeit the use of some nonverbal implicatures — body position and applied attention make up much of the art of suasion. Occasionally, putting people's imaginations into play is even better. Lack of body signals is an implicature all in itself. Voice only, I could rely on my diction and lexicon and see what happened. An office building midway along my route seemed the most promising, so I tapped them.

"The Renior, how can we serve you," came through the tiny speakers in my ears. The voice was flat, computer generated, using English the way my caller profile instructed.

"Security, please," I said back.

Larry's monitor lit up with an old candlestick of a man in a black, nylon mesh shirt. The shirt had padding on the right shoulder, where he might press a rifle butt. I couldn't see the kickback of anything bigger than a paintball not putting this man on his ass. He couldn't see me at all.

"The Renior watch. Over."

"I need exterior surveillance feed from last night."

"All pulls come through legal."

"I need some speed, if you copy."

"You on the job?"

"Negative. This is personal."

"You in personnel? Then you know you've got to reach out to legal. Union rules, partner. What's your ID?"

Forging a positive connection with this guard would take a lot of time. More than one session, probably. I tapped out. The man looked miffed as the screen swallowed itself,

showing me the map again. The first street I'd sprinted down
had three more commercial buildings that might have filmed
my pursuers. The first was owned by a holding company in
Denmark. They wanted nothing to do with me. The second
housed an insurance company that got real spooked by my
questions. The third never answered the voice call. I dictated
a formal request, but I got the sense that it would be read by
automated filters and automated filters alone.

Guessing from the map, as I turned the corner, I passed
an automotive customizer. The kind of place that will outfit
your ride in orange leather, smoothie dispensers, and enough
treble and bass to jellify your eardrums. I'd never talked to
one of these places before. They were merchants, though.
That meant a natural willingness to bargain. I searched
through a farrago of industry info to see what this world did
behind closed garage doors. After twenty minutes of reading
about mood lighting, natural turf, and argon soundproofing,
I punched their button.

"Yellow," a young man answered, voice only.

"I need a favor."

"Spray."

"You got cameras mounted on the exterior of the shop?"

"Yeah."

"You still holding the file from last night?"

"You a cop or some such?" the guy asked.

"Not," I replied. "Two heavy hammers tried to pound me
out after hours, front end of your place."

"Do I know you?"

My use of his trade creole must have been good enough
for him to think I associated with his craft. It could work, so
long as I didn't make him feel like he was being conned.

"Nope. I'm a converter. With solid memory, should you
need a hook up. I'll trade out this favor down the road. Today,
I need to keep this build simple and clean."

"I don't think I want to open this up."

"No feedback," I said. "This is not a cluster. More like a
glitch."

The young man paused. I heard him force air out his
nose. He couldn't figure out what would cause him the least

number of problems — ending this exchange or zipping me the video.

"I know what you're thinking," I said. "Why do you want to add a wrench to some shadetree's hack job, right? A third set of hands under the hood never helps. This is not like that. It blows that this went down near your shop. I'm offering that this can blow by. Two clicks. Send to this phone."

My turn to pause. I listened hard to the silence.

"Fine," the man said. "You caught me shinning."

"You ever need a converter, you let me know."

"It happens." He chuckled to himself. "I'll store your tag."

Eight minutes later the video file arrived on my phone. The images weren't terrible. The shop had better cameras than the city police. The deep purple soup of the night, in the spotty light, made rushing through the footage like watching a Kinescope. Broken, strobing movements, unnatural and macabre. Last night looked like last century, and more frightening for it. My heartrate picked up. I saw myself, running, mouth too wide to plug with a grapefruit. I saw the dark suits chase after me, insulted, pissed off, and determined. They were ill dressed for a serious workout. Under the streetlights, their faces, contorted from their exertion, glowed bone white.

I circled their images, copied, pasted and sent the best of the bunch to Larry.

More waiting, more coffee and finally, more Larry.

"Query additional graphics?" He sounded angry over the phone, but too angry for me to believe he really meant it.

"No," I returned. "Query ID?"

"Your request is fried. Will, stop. End."

"Final run. Complete. My query is critical. No query if false. Honest."

"These graphics scraped last night?"

"Yes."

"They crash your face."

"Approximately."

"Looping, looping, loo—" He signed off. I imagine he'd started thinking of ways to run facial recognition identification routines Trojan Horsed into his current workload. I hoped, anyway. I really wanted to know more about my assailants. Andrea's phone call resulted in a net loss of data.

The last data set I'd downed from Larry had a spike. I didn't forget that tidbit. It gnawed at me, a guilt-driven beaver with a taste for my brainstem. Part of me didn't give a damn, the other part knew Andrea told me the truth.

Over leftovers — a species of broccoli casserole I'm betting Lawrence wished had died off — I caught up on the news headlines selected for me:

Controversy continues around '...' new wordhood.

The Nuclear Air Transport Act debate underway.

The hottest summer on record continues.

I think I read something. Nothing made it out of short-term memory. Lingering thoughts intermixed with the new material, diluting, tainting, reformulating the incoming messages so much that they felt old and unworthy somewhere between the eyes and ears and brain. Nuclear Andrea? Trading Bremburg's meeting? ... you're fired?

Larry called back. The big screen on the wall showed just his name.

"Sending the files. Crossed everything I could. Don't contact me any more today."

"If you could just—" The screen went back to news. I smirked. I didn't really have anything else. I popped open the files.

The modern world's transparency is wonderful until so many layers of fact upon fact make things opaque again. Larry did his best to raise the cream of his data, but he had little idea of my tastes. Although his 'little idea' may have been more than I had.

The digest of his data went: the thugs who tried to kill me were Joshua Chu and Morning Haggerty, staff writers employed by EDP Logistics. The company had a murky mission statement, involving getting stuff done. Stuff. Writers. These are clutch words, useful to interpreters because they are nearly useless to everyone else. Their nebulous meanings are left to interpretation, as we wish all things would be. They were plaster to me, spread on this company documentation to hide cracks in their façade.

All the knowledge in the world is but a few taps away. You just need to know when and where to tap. I ain't the Fred Astaire of research, so I settled in for a grueling routine. Slowly I learned.

Loam did not appear to be one of EDP's clients. None of his various companies or holdings interacted with EDP. EDP had just three clients, Novi Disposal being the only one that seemed to be paying. Novi owned landfills across North America and a fleet of trucks, trains and Zeppelins to keep the dumps engorged. They had a history of legal actions, investigations, and cloudy out-of-court settlements longer than I could stay awake to read. None of which stopped them from acquiring a license to transport nuclear waste.

Nuclear again. Yes, coincidences are mathematical certainties. Despite my text-heavy education, I knew that much. I also knew the intelligence curating my news feeds could see patterns on spectrums I could not. As in, those two parallel lines are parts of a trapezoid, if you trace the ultraviolet sides too. Nuclear energy, nuclear plant, nuclear waste, nuclear hazard.

One of the hazards of interpreting is also faced by backhoe operators, linemen, and ferryboat captains. Routine builds complacency leading to trouble. Interpreters who spend too much time with the same clients, conversing in the same language, can develop expectations. Example: This client uses the word *judgment* after the word *summary* so often her interpreter starts stringing them together whether he hears them or not. Which, on the day she says, "summary proceeding," makes everyone stumble and the interpreter look foolish. I've been trained to detect and avoid this pitfall of my profession. Using this training outside my profession? It never occurred to me. I need to fight expectations. I needed to — against my mother's teachings — stop fighting my personal computer.

I consume news in my car, during my commutes. On occasion, I'll catch a post on a large monitor. My phone, my car, and my house frame all know what I like: English language journalism regarding interpreters, Zeppelin accidents, vintage hip hop, baseball, and very little else. I don't have time for the wide world. I can barely stay on top of the news I need. Language evolution — new pidgins were born every day — new words, old words brought back, structures, usage, theory, not to mention the business side of things.

Summary: laws regarding the transportation of nuclear waste never crossed my desk.

Judgment: I moved around this town like a hamster in a ball of my own making. But something I'd run over had altered the boundaries of my recommended news to include the Nuclear Air Transport Act. A pattern I couldn't see quite yet.

I blew out my search filters and allowed my algorithmic assistant to reach beyond the ports I normally sailed. The search put me in places I'd never seen before.

A plethora of posts appeared in the late spring, screaming at the New York State Legislature. People begged their representatives not to push through legislation allowing spent fuel from nuclear power plants to be transportation by lighter-than-air vehicles. All these people were scientists, so no one listened. Nobody reposts the rants of biologists and physicists. The language is thick, the topics are difficult, and, in the end, people don't care for what they have to say.

It occurred to me that this went beyond the mire of science. This had a political angle.

I drifted into news posts favored by the conservative right. All the blood-and-guts, business first, 'the government should be three guys paying the navy' types. Not ports I usually visit. Nothing showed up. No complaints, no bragging. No chatter at all. Every piece of legislation had a ying and yang. Sides. Somebody had to hate this deal as much as some others liked it. So I threw my net over the starboard side. Maybe the liberal lefties had opinions. After an hour of trolling, I came up empty. I got a few hits on a bill number, discovered that it was being debated right now in special session, and was expected to slip through the Capital like a greased mackerel.

Tomorrow it would be legal to cart nuclear waste through the sky and bury it in various places across the state. Huh. Outside of the League of Concerned Scientists, none of the news outlets I searched were overly concerned with this change in the law, the debate, the rush, or the expected results.

I sat back in Larry's desk chair, eyes unfocused on his family-room wall, with that sensation you get the first time you fly, when you're in an aircraft above the clouds and everything's pure and sunny and you nose down through the fluff and see a busy, sprawling quilt of green and gray splotches. In your lonely, silent, sanitized fugue you view for the first time, firsthand, what a chaotic, patchwork mess we've made of the world. All the demarcation. Property lines, fences, walls, division. Can't say as I cared for it, can't say I did not, as it would be hypocritical. I lead an insular life. I didn't care about nuclear power, or the many other things I didn't know about, understand, or worse — had all wrong.

Of my more immediate worries, this unpeeling left me nothing into which I could sink my teeth. Haggerty and Chu had no discernable interest in me, let alone one strong enough to motivate late night chases and the pulling of guns. I needed a cop. Luckily, one wanted to meet me. Out of the way, and off the record. Perfect.

I felt dumb. The kind of dumb you get from taking a short cut down a dark alley or lighting a match to find a gas leak. Dumb that ends in regret.

Chapter 15

From "Tales without Interpreters"
The chef had been out of work for some time, so he took
a temporary job with a landscaper. The foreman told the
chef his first assignment was to seed the lawn. "Seed a
whole lawn?" the chef repeated, believing this had to be
some kind of prank on the new guy. "Don't make me say
it twice," the foreman growled. Screw this, the chef said to
himself. Seeding a tomato was hard enough. A lawn? He
quit on the spot.

"**—Once more line** to the port,
    Compatible nodes, once more;
    Or shutdown the block with our English fried.
    Inactive there's nothing so coded a user
    As base downtime and organic interface
    But present realtime war audio tones in our monitors
    Then clone the tiger,
    Enable the servos, call up the power
    Mask the program hardware rage.
    Then serve the optical input a spiked byte,
    Allow to run the boards of the processor
    Like the brass canon, allow initialization of the frame—"
The actor had talent. Under the duress of extreme
heat and humidity, exacerbated by the sixty pounds of
chainmail and robes, he pulled off a compelling King
Henry V, more than adequate for someone who probably
understood a tenth of what he said. That is not to say
actors are stupid, they just can't learn every argot is all. I
usually can't brook Shakespeare in anything but English,
and sob like a lawn sprinkler when I hear it in Cyber,

but this evening I figured I'd better save all my tears for myself.

The gates of Harfleur were realistic projections and the sound effects, though not overpowering, had the force to make me cringe with each explosion. But that was me. I cringe easy. Especially when I expect to be picked off by a sniper any moment, the sound of his deadly rifle shot hidden in the clamor of the play. I saw that in a movie once.

The air hung heavy and tacky and dirty. Young lovers didn't cuddle during the performance. They sat on their blankets, adjusting the settings on their wine glasses to make them cooler and cooler, toweling off the sweat that collected on the outside so they wouldn't spill all over their cheese. It was not the best night to hang out with twelve hundred people I didn't know, praying that the one I did know didn't show.

I stood at the back of the audience, even though the cab had dropped me off in plenty of time to get a prime spot on the grass. It would have ruined the play for everyone to see my chest explode from a high-velocity bullet. So, I did what I thought polite; I put my back against a tree. The classic gun-fighter-watching-Shakespeare-in-the-park-position.

Detective Bremburg should have made his entrance before the third act. The waiting made Larry's borrowed clothes stick to me in more and more places. The jeans and a blue, cotton button-down hadn't fit well to begin with. The sneakers had already been relegated to yard work. When it comes time for a snake to slither out of its old skin — this must be what the urgency feels like.

"Kirst." The voice was light-hearted and unexpected.

I turned to see Bremburg, relaxed in a white sport-shirt and chinos, holding a blanket, a six-pack sized cooler and a nylon sport purse — exactly the type you'd expect on the shoulder of an action-hero urban cowboy. He had a huge smile, the kind used when your buddy meets you in a bar he hates.

"Sorry about the clock. The job ran late." He unfurled the blanket.

Hiding the confounded look on my face was pointless and yet I put some effort into it. I didn't know what the night would bring, though beverages had not been on the list. Was this a date?

"How is the show?" His diction and delivery were odd, like he should have been up on the stage, and getting some coaching.

"Fine. The civilian playing Henry is seasoned."

"The actor?" His look underlined the word. The emphasis, while sounding like a question, was what interpreters call dilogical. He put out two pieces of information with one word. In this case, that the man on the stage was an actor and the man saying the word did not want to sound like a cop. Words like civilian, which signaled a security tongue, were out.

"The actor, yes."

"Cold one."

"Oh God yes."

He grinned, lifted the lid of the cooler and drew two frosty cans of Labatt beer. Bremburg cracked a can, and a fizzing hiss was released with a nice, clear, single meaning. He handed me an open one.

"This'll last all of thirty seconds," I said.

"It is a thick one, tonight."

He leaned back against the tree and slurped some beer. The way he placed his purse next to his leg made me apprehensive. I figured it held a gun and he wanted it close. He appeared to be watching the play unless you watched his eyeballs closely. His gaze went over and over the crowd, reading each person like a word. I could almost hear the chug of his internal database. Could that skell be packing? Did I book that kid two years ago for possession? I liked watching him more than the play.

"Faced with brass today, Kirst." His voice lowered and came out the side of his mouth. The words *face* and *brass* alerted me to a more official conversation and his volume told me this exchange would be covert. "Your name came down," he paused, "with questions."

"What kind of questions?"

"Details, involvements, records, the whole locker."

"I don't copy."

"Me neither."

"What did you spill?"

He gave me a disapproving look. "My file on you's about two tips long. What would I spill?"

"Sorry."

"You possess something to spill?" He looked back out towards the stage. "Something you want to unload? Off the record?"

I had lost track of what act or scene played out on the stage. At that moment, I couldn't have followed Shakespeare if I'd been strapped to his back. It occurred to me that maybe Bremburg didn't need as much actor-coaching as I might have thought. He could be trying a friendly interrogation before throwing me in a steel box with a halogen lamp and shouting at me until I busted like a wine glass. I saw that in a movie, too.

"Why this face, detective?" If he was playing a part, I wanted to see how well.

"Brass says you go deeper than the file."

"Sure." I took a swig of the best beer I've ever had. "But you didn't haul me down to the house and put me in a room. That don't connect."

"You fail to copy." He turned, so he could look me in both eyes. "They pulled your file. You are out of bounds."

That policeman stare went right through my eyes and into my gut. Bremburg didn't need an interrogation cell. He did just fine in the middle of a crowd, in the heat and the histrionics. I stared back, holding myself together — a pot I caught as it hit the ground, cracked but with all my pieces still in place. I didn't like being the subject of police politics, discussions, rules — anything, really.

"Why you playing me?" I asked.

"You play what you're dealt."

"You've got nothing else? No other leads?"

"The case is progressing."

"I'm looking like the weakest brick in the wall."

"You looked like you might want to face outside the house is all." His smile slid back into place. "No cameras. No mics."

We watched the play as the sun took its final bow.

"Kirst," he said after a pause long enough for twenty lines of soliloquy, "I respect the oath."

"But...." I tried to start him off. Get him talking. He had that sorry-I-have-to-lock-you-up tone.

"There are circumstances by which—" he said.

"Empty," I stopped him. "No exigency. No ticking time bombs."

"There's something." He sipped his Labatt, panning the crowd. "You aware we're under surveillance?"

What? That wasn't an answer. "Blue?"

"Negative."

Not the cops. OK. "Loam's?"

"Possible. Rookie, though. Not a top dollar tag."

I fought the urge to start looking around. It would enlighten our shadow to that fact that we were no longer in the dark.

"You positive?" I asked.

"The job."

That wasn't an answer either. This guy was full of no answers. "How'd he know we'd be here? Who's he surveilling, me or you?"

"He covers when you scan, so I'm thinking he's on you."

At least I had a cop around this time, presumably with a pistol and everything. I might get caught in a crossfire, but I wouldn't be jumping in shrubs tonight. A step up for me.

The reason for this meeting remained absent. Bremburg didn't strike me as the type of guy who refused to miss a performance of Henry V even if it meant he had to hold a criminal investigation in the park. He wanted to talk to me, and not around other police. His bosses had taken an interest in me, a mystery reinforcing his hunch that I could solve his other mysteries for him.

If I opened my mouth.

Which I had no intention of doing. Not for him, not for the other guy watching us. Not for nothing.

"What's the deal, detective? I'm out-of-bounds but here you are. Face to face."

"Olivia Carl's dad. We got him in the cooler. Between you, me, and the tree, he never discharged a firearm in his life. I can't clear this case. I ain't never going to clear this case. This case will remain open in my file until I'm replaced by some robot monkey cop and he ain't never going to clear it, either."

I stopped pretending to be watching the stage and turned my head to look at him. I had to see what kind of face went with an answer like that. He took a swig of brew and maintained the appearance of a man discussing the night's humidity.

"Sorry," I said.

"Ten four, partner. You're on your own job now."

Bremburg's superiors sent word down to stay away from me. I had protection, of a sort. That should've been comforting, but the comfort eluded me. I didn't like the thought of letting a killer go free and an innocent man doing time for it. I didn't like people talking about me, either. People somewhere, sliding comments back and forth, about me and my mouth. Watching me, to make sure I kept it closed.

"You try the posts?" I asked.

"B Carlisle covered my beat, evening in question. Know them?"

"Secondary association."

"Empty." Bremburg stretched his neck and rolled his head around a bit, trying to pop out the kinks. Then he looked me in the eyes again. "Worse than empty. They fingered Olivia Carl's dad, then dropped the case."

"You question them about that?"

"Negative."

What a silly question. The posts in Beau Fleuve were a loose association of people self-labeling as reporters. New York State didn't make you register in any way. You've got to get a license to paint fingernails. Reporting? Illuminating society, helping people better understand their world, ensuring a transparent government and corporate responsibility? Anybody can do that. All that matters is getting read. The truth is but one, little-used prop in that show.

Professional reporters — the people clever enough to make a living observing and relaying — tend to know a handful of languages. They are cousins to interpreters from the side of the family we don't like to talk about. Their relationships tend to be give and take, take, take. I know when it comes to the police, they might give a little more than usual because there are times when there's a good deal to take. Standard, nightly beat crime is not one of those times. Those stories are stuffing, not the turkey. B Carlisle didn't understand this one, though. This Dombrowski murder had the makings of a full Thanksgiving meal.

Bremburg almost understood. I gave him credit for hanging in there, for not obediently dropping the vagrant in prison and moving on to the next case. He believed himself to be at a dead end, a *clue de sac*, and so desperate he took a shot at turning me. He knew a bigger story hid around the corner, even as he spun in circles.

Like every profession, interpretation has its own argot. We have, for example, the *oink* derived from the abbreviation ONC or Oration of No Consequence. This is frequently a bit of small talk or a joke an interpreter may repeat later, even though he or she heard it in the course of duty. And we have the LIC, Lapse in Confidentiality. While they are most often honest mistakes, like interpreters momentarily forgetting where they heard some tidbit or flake of gossip, the consequences can be serious. I hoped to place my next comment in the middle. Between an oink and a lic.

"What do you know about the Quarantine Zone?"

Bremburg glanced at me, not bothering to hide his curiosity. "It's the scene of a crime, why?"

"No. Really," I said. "Run it down."

"It is mostly on Tuscarora Rez. Not even State Troopers go in or out."

"You're yanking me, right?"

"Negative. It is a jurisdictional dead zone."

"I read that it was empty."

"Empty like an abandoned building," Bremburg said. "Rookie year you learn to clear every corner or rookie year is your only year."

"You think there's corners to clear on the Rez?"

"No intelligence on that. We're never allowed to gather any."

"So, you don't like the scene because it's a locked box."

"Everyone's got a closet," Bremburg said. "And every closet's got something in it."

A closet? Specifically, I think he meant the kind that contains skeletons. My mouth started spouting before my brain thought better of it. "There is a rehabbed Zeppelin rig on the Rez." I blushed. It felt like I'd just explained a dirty joke.

Bremburg failed to contain his surprise. His eyes remained pointed at the players taking their final bows. His mind put on a whole other show.

People stood and applauded and began packing coolers and rolling blankets with the foolish hope of getting a spot on the road before the other cars crammed it up.

"Male, cauc, six-foot, brown hair, jeans and a red shirt." Bremburg continued to smile and clap enthusiastically.

"Where?"

"Three o'clock."

I looked to my right and got a peek. The muscular man stood facing the stage.

"He's not one of them," I said to myself, but out loud.

"One of who?" Bremburg asked.

"Them." I'd said too much and not enough. "Two assailants, last night. I was accosted in front of my premises, approximately twenty-one-hundred hours. I called in to report it."

"To who?"

"You," I answered. "We got sideways."

"My apologies," Bremburg said. "We cross and split. Rendezvous forward of the museum. I'll spot you." He leaned in and gave me a hug. I stiffened. Fake, awkward, ruining the performance. He walked off past the man who pretended not to watch us.

I sifted into the crowd, hunching, willing myself shorter and thinner. I wanted to shrink from telling Bremburg about the tower. I'd never come close to oinking, let alone licking, at any time in my career. The herd moved at a third the speed I wanted. The red-shirted man stalked behind me. My shoulders tingled. I shuffled with the throng, waiting for a hand to land there, on the tingles, talons forcing me in a new and terrible direction.

The crowd slowed more, confused, a few hurried up, parting in a great V. Lights flashed. A white sedan rolled on the grass, red and blue strobes blasting. People slammed their eyes closed, threw their arms across their faces, and stumbled out the way. Except for me. The car stopped sideways and the door blew open.

"Get in." Bremburg leaned across the seat. A trackless cop-cruiser. I smiled for the first time in three days. I jumped in as he righted himself. We peeled off the sidewalk before the door gave the cozy click of a good seal. I thanked Bremburg for not dumping me out of a moving car so soon after rescuing me. He tugged the big joystick that jutted from the floor in the center of the car, worked the speed-trigger, and continued to ignore me.

Bremburg piloted the sedan into the road and into the traffic with acumen. He maneuvered over the track and lowered the till into the slot, but didn't switch the vehicle to full-auto. We weren't even going to tell the car where we were headed.

He activated the information system on the dash and turned on the glo-map. The green and blue lights filled the interior of the car and my heart thunked.

"Kirst," Bremburg said, adjusting the brightness of the monitor, "you note the scene of the Zep rig?"

I pulled out my phone. I'd saved everything.

He repeated the demarcation out loud and the map on the dashboard changed its display. A new map showed the best way to get from our current locale to Loam's recent acquisition. Then brilliant, red letters crawled across the face of the screen, drowning out the pleasant green and blue hues.

—Tuscarora Reservation: Authorized access only. Tuscarora Reservation: Authorized access only—

Bremburg said nothing. I assumed that the message had dissuaded him from visiting the area and he was contemplating what to do next. I chose to be quiet and let him pick a new destination. I certainly didn't have anything intelligent to add. I looked at all the wonderful gadgets in the car, all of the orange, green, red, and blue lights striving to report their significance.

We zipped down another ramp and onto another section of the Thruway. We were headed due north and moving like we had a reason.

"Bremburg, are we cruising?"

"No. We've got a call."

"I didn't copy—"

"Nighttime reconnaissance."

We drove off into the stale night, pointed at a place we did not belong. Driving away from Shakespeare in the Park, the words of Henry V lingered in my mind.

"Once more unto the breach," I said.

Chapter 16

From "Tales without Interpreters"
The marketing executive explained to his banker that he
needed to promote his new product at trade shows. He
needed another loan to create collateral. The banker said
he needed more collateral before he could have another
loan.
"I can't produce any collateral without a loan," the
marketer said. To which the banker replied, "you can't use
a loan for collateral." This continued as the new product
floundered from lack of visibility, the business folded, and
the banker lost his initial investment.

"What's with the ride along?" I said into the sole of Bremburg's green and white cross-trainer.

"You're saying one thing, I'm saying another." His voice
came from under the dashboard of the unmarked police car.
The penlight in his mouth bounced as he spoke, running
streaks of blue-white light across the car's headliner.

"And you think we need to be in step right now?" I asked.

Upside-down, one leg over the back of the seat, the other
bent like it might kick me, head and shoulders on the floor,
he declined to answer right away. I turned to look out the
window at the cars jetting by. I'd never been on the side
of the road before. Things — vehicles, I presumed — were
roaring blurs chased by lightning.

Ah, the joys of the trackless. Every boy's dream. To yank
up the tiller and jerk to the side of the road in complete
control of your own speed and direction and destiny. It's
a romantic freedom. To be a cowboy. Ripping up mud and
grass. No boundaries. No rules. No deference to others. It's

the main reason people choose to become law enforcement officials and don't let them tell you otherwise.

If this were nothing more than an aimless amble in the country, I would have enjoyed the ride. Bremburg had a target, though. It was not a hit with me.

"I don't want to investigate the Rez," I said.

"The rap is worse than the record." He rattled and wriggled under the dash, as he had been for the last ten minutes.

"Ten minutes ago you said your report on the Rez was empty," I protested.

"That don't mean hazardous."

"Why bring me? I'm no use to you."

"You were already riding shotgun," Bremburg said. "Besides, a mouthpiece can be handy."

He may have meant that as a compliment or he may have been justifying his choice to kidnap me. It is tough to read a face when it's contorted and visible only in arrhythmic flashes.

"Handy," I repeated. "Like pepper spray or handcuffs?"

"Can you incapacitate with your jabbering?" he asked.

"I once stunned two ninjas with a single, well-placed preposition."

"Busted," Bremburg said with a hint of triumph. He rocked himself out from under the dash and flipped right-ways. Then he held up what looked like an olive slice with two steel blades jutting out of the sides, and smiled.

I said, "Was that blocking off the mood lighting?"

"Global positioning system signal. Now suspended."

The City of Beau Fleuve Police Department could no longer whisper into their computers and locate this car. A dubious, unsettling accomplishment.

Bremburg started the vehicle moving, picked his space and easily merged with the traffic. Due to the time of night, and the direction we were heading, there weren't that many cars on the road.

"We're way off the record now," I said. "Won't headquarters be suspicious about the car going missing?"

"Equipment failure," He replied. "It happens with regularity."

"Why do you want to check out the rig right now," I said.

"They didn't rehab it for the squirrels."

Twenty minutes later we turned down a fire-road. No more tracks. Broken pavement, potholes, patches of rusted iron rebar hidden in weeds and tall, floppy grass. Even as we slowed to four miles-per-hour, the dislodged chunks of concrete made the car bounce and buck. The beams of the headlights traced wild arcs on the brush.

Ten minutes after negotiating the fire-road, we stopped. In the distance stood a gate fifteen feet high, covered in bright, but peeling, yellow paint. The signs bolted on pylons displayed red slashed out circles and read: *Tuscarora Reservation — Authorized-Certified-Licensed Access-Admission-Line Only.*

Simple enough, I thought.

"The sign says we need clearance."

"See, I knew a mouthpiece would be handy. Thanks."

He squeezed the joystick. My head knocked back into the seat; my eyes cranked opened wide to take in all of the disbelief. We aimed at the center of the gate. The car jostled up and down and side-to-side, knocked from crevasse to boulder and back. Bremburg's bloodless hand clenched the quivering stick, a fist strangling an angry snake. Twice we heard the metallic shrieks of the car floor bottoming out.

Forty miles-per-hour. That gate looked solid enough to kill us.

Fifty miles-per-hour. I laughed, remembering that I thought Bremburg would protect me from getting wacked by gangsters.

Sixty miles-per-hour. The rocketing sedan plowed through the gates before I could get my hands fully in front of my face. The sound scraped my ears.

Bremburg let up on the trigger and gradually pulled back on the joystick, engaging the brakes. The car decelerated without traumatic side-ways skidding. We continued down the road-like path as if the fencing had been a Dr. Pepper can. There were no sounds of residual damage.

We drove for another fifteen minutes, winding on what used to be a road, through rubbish, cracks, and pits large enough to swallow a cow. Oaks and elms on either side formed a black tunnel over us. They cut us off from the sky. From everything. Bremburg paid close attention to the glomap and made several turns. My interest waned as I became disoriented. My mouth had lost all its moisture back at the gate. I felt like a tuning fork.

He stopped the cruiser in the middle of the road.

"Are we there yet, Dad?" I asked. Through the side window I saw nothing but gnarled foliage.

"Negative." He motioned outside as he opened his door.

Steamy air blew in. I had forgotten how preferable the air conditioning had made things inside the cruiser. Leaving the clement car didn't strike me as a great idea. Still, I snapped the latch and left.

Bremburg stood with his back to me looking through the trees, up into the sky. I followed his line of sight to the end of the road where the trees thinned, then up. Despite the blackness, I could make out the ridged, manmade lines of a tall, narrow rectangle. It had a brim near the top. A crane wearing a top hat. The Zeppelin tower.

I turned to Bremburg. "How far to the rig?"

"Ten minutes," he answered.

Bremburg used his phone's light to check the underside of the car. He apparently didn't see anything of concern. We got back in and he started it crawling over the swathe of pavement and weeds we'd been following through the forest.

We soon stopped again, but this time I knew why. Dull, yellow lights emanated up ahead. They put out enough glow to let you guess at the structures. Sheds or shanties, it looked like, made from wood, concrete, and corrugated steel. As my research listed the Quarantine Zone as uninhabited, the warm gentle glow of the summer lights gave me a serious chill.

"Report?" I asked.

"No clue." He turned off the sedan, then reached under his seat and brought up his purse. The sound of a zipper can be tantalizing. This was not. I didn't want to go anyplace where he wanted to wear a gun.

His pistol was hearse black, laid out in a matching Kevlar shoulder holster. He donned the rig and then reached back for his wallet. Out came his bright silver shield, which he fastened to the left shoulder strap of his rig.

Westerns, detective shows, movies about corporate spies, or any past war, are fine with me. I love watching actors with guns. Real people? Not so much. Bremburg's piece of ceramic and thermal plastic, locked and loaded, ready to spit hot lead with the thinnest of thoughts, made me uneasy. The mystique the pistol once held for me had dissipated when that last one was leveled at my head.

Bremburg drew his pistol, checked it over as it made some clicky noises, and shoved it back into place.

"What's the deal with the firearm?"

"What's the deal with the domestic up ahead?" He stared down the road. "I'm going investigate the scene. Hang rear."

And do what? Listen to some light jazz? I didn't want to go with Bremburg, but I had an equal desire not to be left alone. It didn't matter that I didn't like guns, I wanted to stick with the guy who had one. We got out and started our stealthy stroll towards the yellow lights.

The brush approached impassable. I couldn't believe so much stuff could grow this thick with this little rain. The region hadn't had a shower in weeks, despite the fact that I could pull a drink right out of the air if I sucked hard enough.

Staying close to the trees, on the side of the crumbling road, we inched toward the nest of buildings. This had once been a minor intersection. A short strip of tiny shops, the comical remains of a gas station. One building had the stance of a saloon and the tepid yellow of electric light ghosted out through moss and grime matted windows. I presumed that's where the ol' sheriff was a headin'. The glow from the pub beckoned like a bug light. We both should've learned from the moths.

I did not have a clear view of our mission out here in a restricted area in the middle of a work night. Telling Bremburg about a Zeppelin tower on the Rez should not have led to a buddy-picture-turned-slasher-movie.

A creaking sound. We crouched in the thick plants. The door of a supposed bar opened, and a skinny male emerged with a long firearm cradled in his arms. There were no streetlights, and the trees blocked what little light the hazy stars and moon offered. All I could say from his silhouette was that his boots were big. Bremburg went still as a statue. He didn't have to tell me not to peep. Two more men emerged from the darkness, walking from the same direction we had come from, but down a path we had not seen. They were young, clomping in big boots, and armed with long guns.

"Box ride, Skid," one of the men said to the man who had just come from the bar.

"No cleans," the other one added.

"Need to be some, dregs. Scoop the clogs and dot the squat."

I couldn't quite make out the argot they were using, but the man from the bar gave orders.

The two scouts walked off to our left, vanishing in the shadows. The leader lingered, looking into the woods. For a moment I thought he looked at us. My breathing stopped. After a painful ninety seconds, he went back into the bar.

Bremburg turned back towards the car without a sound. I followed, still holding my breath. A little farther back into the woods Bremburg stopped me with a firm grasp of my shoulder. He brought his face well inside my ear and whispered, "Pull back solo if I don't make the rendezvous."

I could hear the seriousness in his voice, though I couldn't discern the source.

"Neg, partner." I would not be leaving without him.

"Orders, Will."

"I'm not under your command." I tried to sound as stern as he had been, without raising my voice.

Bremburg bowed his head for a second, summoning patience I assumed. I'd seen the posture before. Boss. Teacher. Second date. He raised his head and said, "Okay."

We continued with as much haste and as little noise as possible. The dead twigs and crinkly leaves fought us all the way. Neither of us had been reared by, well, people who could move about the woods in silence. Luckily, the car sat just a hundred feet away — one hundred, lightless, noisy, wide-open feet away.

At the brink of the road we stopped again. Bremburg drew his pistol and held it pointed at the ground. He put his other hand on my shoulder and pushed me lower. We both squatted in the cusp of the brush.

Squatted. What had that man said? Dot the squat?

The car waited alone. We saw no armed guard or another vehicle or anything at all that would impede our departure. Bremburg's eyes zipped and darted, hitting on every glint of light and hint of movement. I had been holding my breath going on a quarter of an hour.

From context, I thought those two younger men were looking for something. Us, I figured. Would you look for a squat? Outside of a gym, I couldn't—

"On three." Bremburg's voice cut through my ruminations.

"Copy that," I returned.

He counted and we ran. I flew to the passenger side of the cruiser, he sort of hopped around the front, turning, watching the full three hundred and sixty degree view, holding his sidearm with both hands. The brief flash of the dome light inside the sedan made me feel vulnerable. The sound of our doors closing was both satisfying and too loud for my liking. Bremburg poked in his ignition code. He looked behind and squeezed the trigger.

The car rocked, the motors wined, but the car refused to roll.

He repunched the reverse key with a quick jab of his fingers and gunned it again. Nothing. We were stuck. He smashed the forward key. The car clanked. The wheels whirled. The vehicle moved not an inch.

I watched him wriggle around in the driver's seat. My hands flapped. I squirmed. My body wanted to help, but I couldn't talk to machines.

"Fly!" Bremburg shouted.

I had no idea what he meant. I think he shouted at the car. He broke open his door and bent out like he'd gotten sick.

"Phone, Kirst!"

He kept his in a side pocket. I slid it out and slapped it into the hand he had thrust across his chest and back at me. He searched under the car.

"Jacks!" he spat out.

He somersaulted out of the car. I nearly ripped the handle off trying to get my own door open. I dropped to the ground and looked under the cruiser. The tire nearest me hovered a wee bit above the ground. A hydraulic floor jack held up the front end. I glanced towards the rear and saw its twin holding up its end.

"Get the front one," Bremburg growled. He shot to standing.

"Right," I growled back, popping up. I could slide, like stealing second, kick the stand out, and the tires wouldn't let the car pin my—

Two crimson flashlights, attached half way up the barrels of two rifles, pointed at me. The light made the guns look hot and molten and prevented me from seeing the faces aiming the weapons.

"Clamps rear of the bucket!" A voice crackled behind the red glare.

"What?" I didn't understand. Nice time to draw a blank, right? His rifle wouldn't.

"Clamps rear of the bucket, clean!"

I didn't move. I didn't speak. I didn't know what this guy wanted.

"Clamps rear of the bucket or I spray!" he yelled.

I couldn't think. I couldn't blink. For the first time in my adult life, I couldn't understand a word being said to me.

Chapter 17

From "Tales without Interpreters"
The accountant asked the real estate developer if he knew
about the variance. The developer assured him that he
was on top of things. The accountant said the variance
bothered him and the developer said it was completely
normal with building in this part of the city. They were
lucky to have it. This made no sense to the accountant.
Coming up two million dollars short never seemed like a
good thing, but he knew he had a lot to learn about the
construction business.

I sat on what felt like a rusted oil drum, clenching my knees
to my chest, shaking. I held my hand in front of my face to
test the old adage, and it held true. Nothing. The totality
of the darkness astounded me. I didn't shake from cold.
The temperature in our little room probably hit a hundred
degrees. As much air got in as light. I shook from withdrawal.
All the hormones, endorphins, and other response-oriented
chemicals your body makes in emergencies are for emergencies only. Because they mess you up if you use them too long.
My third night of chases, lies, guns, imprisonment, and the
fact that I couldn't communicate with my captors, turned my
nerves into frazzled, sparking wires. My imminent autopsy
would unleash live cables on whomever performed it, my
guts whipping around the poor pathologist's lab in a bright
blue electrical shower.

This would only happen if they found my body. An absurd
thought. These yahoos were going to dip Bremburg and me in
boiling acid vicious enough to render dental records useless.
They would dribble our bubbling dregs into—

The yahoos used the word *dregs*. The leader said something about dregs. I wished I had recorded everything on my phone. I wished I had my phone. They took it, of course. They — the people who weren't supposed to be here, in a deserted patch of land. No one lives in the Quarantine Zone. Everyone knows that. Now including me, thanks to the previous night's research. And where did all the Tuscarora go when the quarantine was declared? Maybe they didn't go anywhere. One mystery solved, I guess ... with another mystery. What were they doing here? Not exactly progress.

Bremburg paced off the dimensions of the cell we were stuck in, and then felt along every inch of the walls and floor. I could hear each vain scrap and shuffle. I remained on the drum only because he hadn't gotten around to exploring the ceiling yet.

"What kind of gear do you carry?" His voice made me jump.

"Gear?" I asked. "Like a flare gun or grappling hook?" I felt around in my pockets. Out came Chapstick, lint, and a twist-tie. That last item being yet another mystery; none of it being the laser blaster he wanted.

"Here," I said, sticking my hands out into the nothing.

"Thanks," he felt around my hands, with more gentle probing than I'd expected. He scooped out the contents like he thought he might scratch me. I hoped I wouldn't need to cinch up a bread bag anytime soon.

My wristwatch had a dial, with a little hand and big hand. It didn't tell me my pulse rate or biofeedback patterns or white-blood cell count. It didn't change color when I felt amorous or project some 3D display of the time a half-inch above the face when I pushed in the crown. It required an external light source and therefore I had no idea how long we had been stuck in the kiln. My guess would have been five years.

"Detective Bremburg," I said, "Time served?"

"Forty minutes." He stood right next to me. Who knew?

"Man, could I bust a beer right now."

"Couldn't stop at one."

It never occurred to me before just how much my life revolved around beverages. I wake to coffee, work with coffee, and try to decide if I should have flat or sparkling water with lunch. I stop for a drink, meet him or her for a drink, catch a ball game with beer, grab a martini with a twist of jazz. Man, did I need a drink. This was not prison. There is a choice of beverages in prison. This was Hell.

Bremburg kicked the wall to my right, the wall opposite the one with the door. No hollow reverberation. It could very well have been six hundred feet thick. He tried the door for the fifth time, then the wall again. I wanted to help with the escape research, but in a room about as long and deep as I was tall, it would have been too intimate for the current temperature and humidity. I decided my job would be consideration of other options. First: were there any? Surrender had already been a shining success. I didn't think we could top it.

There were more than a few questions moseying about my mind. Our captors could have shot us at the car or in the woods. Nobody would have seen or heard. Instead, they were actually quite congenial. I took this to mean they didn't know what to do with us. They caught us, but they couldn't eat us or throw us back, so they threw us in this cooler.

I had seen the business end of four rifles, which I assumed meant at least four people. Whether this included the three men from the bar, I couldn't say. Our captors never manhandled Bremburg or me, or spit on us or anything. They just motioned us along through the woods, threatening to shoot, but never pulling a trigger. I didn't get a look at their faces and didn't think Bremburg could have either. Sweat drenched T-shirts and boots. Not much else entered my visual memory.

Visual memory would not be my choice for the talent portion of the competition. My skills, such as they were, came from the verbal regions of the brain.

"Clamps rear of the bucket, clean!" they had said to me. I could still hear them shouting it at me, ruby-red glare and dead black rifle barrels punctuating the sentence. I repeated it over and over in my head. I couldn't get the whole of the meaning and felt my life depended on figuring it out. The argot that they were using was foreign to me, and without sounding arrogant, that is rare. I kept abreast of the latest colloquialisms and official new words. I *subscribed to Cants Can, Voyage of the Argot, and Patois*. The interpreter business is slick and fluid, every new profession can lead to a new pidgin, then creole, then even a language. Still, they all started with the mother tongue. Thanks to English I could fake my way through almost any conversation. With this one, I was in the dark. On a drum.

"Move." Bremburg had crept up next to me again.

I dropped down from my drum and listened to him climb on top. He clawed high at the wall and knocked on the ceiling. The sound told me we wouldn't get wet if it rained tonight.

Clean, I had heard twice. The first time from the leader, the second time it came from whomever pointed a rifle at me. I sensed a pejorative noun, despite the positive association of the source word. It had been directed at Bremburg and me, and it had differentiated us from those using the term. I decided a *clean* must be someone from outside their cohort.

The words now coming out of Bremburg I had heard lots of times before. They were fairly universal. Nothing new to add to my collection. He hopped down from the partially filled can, causing a sloshing sound. This meant that a fair portion of the toxins inside had leaked out into the room over the past however many years and were now working their way into my pancreas.

"The cell's tight," Bremburg said. "We'll need another plan of escape."

"Attempted screaming. We haven't perpetrated that yet."

"Hey!" He began pounding on the door with both fists. "Hey! I want the OI!"

I had been kidding when I suggested screaming. Bremburg sounded uncharacteristically desperate.

"Hey you! Skells!" He continued to pound. The din of the metal door against the doorframe stabbed my ears. "I want to face!"

"Bremburg." I tried to get my voice over the thunder.

"Hey!" he continued.

"Bremburg! Maybe I should take the bullhorn, eh?"

He stopped. "Are you louder than me?"

"No. I make more sense. They won't copy a word you're putting out."

I moved towards the sound of his voice and we both started to pound on the door. We weren't lacking in volume.

"Dregs!" I remembered hearing that word. The leader had used it, and it wasn't *cleans*. "We want to talk."

I had no idea if English would work any better than Security, but it sounded less authoritarian. The sentence had low complexity, the kind of simple phrase that crosses cants.

Boom.

One of the guards hit the door with something much denser than flesh. A rifle-butt would have been my guess.

"Plug it," a man on the other side grunted.

I fumbled my way back to the canister and sat down. The door hadn't thrown a single punch at us, but I felt like it won the fight. By sound alone, I could tell Bremburg could not sit still.

"At ease, officer," I said. "We've got to wait this out."

I wanted to sit and shake some more. The physical exertion involved in beating on a large slab of steel had been good for my nerves, but not my hands or ears.

"Yes," Bremburg replied. "Get some sleep."

That would be harder than breaking out of the joint. I had to keep my mind diverted, but not digressive. If I tried to fall asleep and started to think about my present situation — waiting to learn if I would die by bullet, acid, or carcinogen — my last three drops of moisture would be lost down my cheeks.

Clamps rear of the bucket. What does that tell me? The tone of voice carrying the message carried punctuation with it. The volume and forcefulness over-powered intonation that would have made the sentence feel like a question.

Clamps rear of the bucket, had been a command. He told me to do something. But Bremburg and I had no clamps or buckets. Had they been real security guards or soldiers I would have expected base, general command forms like *freeze* or *hold it*. There are a few universal terms everyone recognizes. Perhaps an older, media driven idiom like *reach for the sky, partner* or *hands in the air*.

Hands. Clamps. Maybe.

Bucket — head? Silly, but "Hands behind your head," worked for me. Clamps were hands, buckets were heads. We were clean, they were dregs. It was a start, like finding a loose stone in the dungeon wall.

Even without the benefit of any sensory perception, I could tell Bremburg's brain chiseled away at our cell. He might be designing a bomb from my Chapstick, calculating the pound-force per square inch needed to break the lock, wondering if this can contained juice caustic enough to eat through the wall, or how long it would take to burrow into the floor like moles. He wouldn't be able to sleep immured in concrete.

I needed to hear more of this new argot. I could begin to build an understanding if I had more blocks of words. Words can build things — walls around people, ramparts encircling colleagues and loved ones, insulating them from others that could be colleagues and loved ones. Words can build lodges and clubhouses for the most discriminating cliques. Words can build capitals and cathedrals and tombs.

What we needed was a road out of here. Words can build those too. Tracked roads. Everyone with their lexicographic tillers plunged deep, guiding them to where they want go and at the same time steering them away from more, new, and undiscovered.

Or keeping them in lightless cells in a place no one would ever think to look. Freedom, it would seem, is quite like tightrope walking. Start with small steps. And practice.

Dregs.

Chapter 18

From "Hoe of Babylon"
The Annual Consensus Evaluation erupted yesterday when the question of acceptance of '...' as a base English word came up for a vote. Dr. Chan Rinesworth vigorously argued against wordhood, stating, "Perhaps, were I a porpoise and could make this sound, it might convey oral meaning. In extant form it is punctuation. That's all it is or ever will be."
Dr. Tamala Boyce rebutted, "The pause has a long and cherished place in spoken exchange. You should try it, Dr. Rinesworth. I mean really give a good, long try."
"I'm not a fish," Rinesworth replied.
"You mean mammal."
"I am one of those. Of the higher functioning kind, that realizes the lack of a word is not, in fact, a word."
"If I may pause for a moment," Dr. Boyce said. "...Fuck you."
"Without hesitation, fuck you," Dr. Rinesworth returned.

"Kirst," Bremburg cracked the silence.

"Yes," I said back into the pitch.

"What are you mumbling?"

"Sorry. I was singing. Rapping, actually. Thought you were asleep."

"You need to restrain yourself. Your noise is cluttering my channels."

"I'd rather be snoring, believe me."

The dead silence returned.

"Rapping?" Bremburg inquired. "Is that music with priors?"

"Wha?" I answered. "Oh, oh, rap as in criminal charge. No. Rap is poetry, with a beat. It's from way back."

"You should put it back."

"Trying to recall the rhymes … it puts me at ease."

"Sounded like you were saying 'fuck the police.'"

"I can … ah … corroborate that."

"What are you saying that for?" Bremburg's voice had a nice mix of irritation and, I think, hurt. Though I might have been a bit too desperate to draw meaning through the black haze, too eager to picture a little wounded Bremburg, as I had not seen anything in hours.

"There was no intent to disrespect," I said. "I like the use of language in those old records. I'm not always complicit in what they're saying, but I love the way it gets said. You copy?"

The blackness filled in, like it wanted to snuff out our tired, grouping sounds.

"Okay," Bremburg said.

My grandfather used to take me fishing up in the northern most portions of Niagara County, up on the streams that ran in from Lake Ontario. The deep lake water made even the shallow slips cold. The salmon and steelhead liked it. Grandpa tied his own flies. He made intricate devices of feather, string, and sharp, barbed hooks. Each lure was bright, enticing, and scavenged. Fuchsia fluff trimmed from an old stuffed animal. Gold thread pulled from a Christmas ribbon. Feathers plucked from a dead blue jay beneath his front picture window. Some flies worked, some didn't. I could never tell. Nothing much bit for me no matter what or where I cast.

Fishing wasn't the point. Spending time with grandpa, that was something. It never took less than an hour to get to whatever fishing spot caught his imagination. We'd ply his Subaru wagon over, into, and out of all kinds of trails and fields and places that reminded me quite a bit of the Quarantine Zone. To the where tracks end. The whole time he would blast his car's sound system, playing the music of his youth.

"Don't tell your mom," he said the first time he cued up one of his favorite songs. It was the best introduction to a piece of music an eleven-year-old could hope for.

"You are now about to witness the strength of street knowledge," Dr. Dre said through the speakers.

—*Straight outta Compton, crazy motherfucker named Ice Cube*

From the gang called Niggas Wit Attitudes—

Ice Cube sang? Spoke? I didn't know. I did know Mom wouldn't approve. So I loved it.

N.W.A, Nas, Wu-Tang Clan, Jay Z — Gramps fed them all to me, from his personal golden age. And I ate it up. The thump, the ferocity, the cleverness and the conviction — it wasn't served to me but flung at me. The tracks were not love songs; they had heft and purpose I'd never heard, not before the hip and the hop of grandpa's car.

The wonderful thing about rap — about any digitized music, really, but with this frozen, old-timey style especially — is that it stays the same forever. Ragtime has had a resurgence, jazz keeps evolving, classical orchestral music gets replayed by each successive generation because it is good or right or — and I lean a little towards this theory — results from arcane magics that entrance the susceptible. Music made by the flinging of words no longer suffers reinterpretation. It has been left to the records. Preserved in its prime for all time. Perpetual.

The same cannot be said of grandpas.

All music has its fans. Musical comedies still get staged, off off-Broadway, shown to the purists who can pay. I gather there is still quite a bit of liturgical music performed on a regular basis. I'm not sure every congregation gets the whole of every message, but that's nothing new.

I went to see a rap revival band last year. With Isla. I thought she might get a charge out of it. A couple of drinks, some loud music, a set of performers doing it for the love. They were so far from selling out they barely broke even each night.

Isla being a lawyer and a woman, and the majority of rap lyrics having to do with the criminal justice system or female body parts, I believed she might appreciate the show. For a little while, it seemed she might. She bounced in place to the beats. She smiled. Then they decided to do N.W.A's "Parental Discretion Advised."

She turned to me and tugged my ear down to her mouth. "You like this shit?"

"It's wild," I said with a smile. "My grandpa introduced me to it."

"Killing police and assaulting woman?"

"It's from like a century ago," I said. "Things were different."

"Yeah," she shouted. "Because we ceased exhibiting this garbage."

"Can I get you another G-and-T?"

With some people, you only remember the bad times. As Isla grew angry her pink lips pressed and rumpled like bed sheets. When you find someone more adorable the madder they get, your relationship sets off on an unsustainable trajectory. Like skydiving, right? It's fun while you're tumbling, then smack. Earth v. knees. Get me out of these straps and help me pack for the next time.

We'd all rather fly, I suppose. Soar on thermals, turning in huge, lazy arcs. The hawks would sail around grandpa and me, on occasion, when we fished. They were free to soar, safe from anything we could muster, and smart enough to know there might soon be fresh fish for the taking.

Smart, safe, free. Stinking up my cell, I admitted, I'm no hawk. Isla once called me a parrot. A pretty bird that sits and repeats. Do the trick well and you get fed. The parrots are not breaking out of their cages and taking wing to the open skies, screeching fear into their prey. No. They sit on a shoulder, quacking comic relief. They are sidekicks, henchmen, secondary players playing far below their intelligence and talent.

I decided right there, on my dark drum, more than a year after Isla said it — I'm no parrot.

Chapter 19

From "Tales without Interpreters"
Captain Lynn Clark was not yet used to being the center of attention. She never set out to be a hero. The psychologist she spoke with said this graduation speech might be a great way to overcome her fear of public speaking. Lynn had her doubts, but she thought she'd start slow, maybe with just the 'Commencement Exercises.' She'd been involved with exercises before. If there was one thing the Marines taught her, it was the benefit of practice.

A disgusting film covered my body. All the previous evening's sweat stuck to me. Dust, dirt, and dung stuck to the sweat. I felt like sandpaper. No, I didn't want sandpaper, as in *I feel like having some sandpaper.* My skin had become sandpaper. Keep the utterances clear, Willy. Words are all you've got.

Specs of light dotted the doorframe, making it less than perfectly black in our cell. More like a deep, dark charcoal. My neck ached from the weird sleeping position. Although I needed water, I would have killed a man with my bare hands for a cup of coffee.

The door's deadbolt slid. I heard Bremburg scramble. The light blasted us. Maybe I'd get my chance at that coffee.

"Pump, cleans. Click to flow."

I assumed this command to be from one of the men who had escorted us in here the night before. Never having seen any of their faces, I couldn't be positive, nor could I really see in the new brightness. I let more light in as my eyes adjusted.

Two men in dirty T-shirts and tall boots stood in the doorway, fingers on the triggers of their long firearms. Rifles or shotguns, I couldn't say. The boys didn't look like they had a better night than I did. They were crumpled and unshaven, but their hair seemed fine and they didn't smell bad. They hadn't completely forsaken the civilized world.

Bremburg sized them up, thinking he might grab for a weapon or dash for the door. I wondered what *pump* meant. In context, it seemed like an action verb.

"Flow. We got a squat collection valved." Our captors waved the gun barrels towards the door. One of them backed out, the other staying behind us.

Firearms, it seems, are even better than coffee when it comes to getting me out the door in the morning.

As we exited, I looked around. When we had entered, the night before, the darkness and thick, red lighting had impaired my view of the place. I could see now that our cell had been impenetrable concrete, with a foot-thick, steel door — familiar, but unplaceable.

I carefully glanced at my watch. No sudden movements. I didn't want my spine blown apart just because I wondered about time. The face said it was a little after nine.

After the hallway I realized we were in a retail store. The shelves hadn't seen so much as a cheese doodle in the last million years. The floor and shelves had turned a yellow that reminded me of the keys on my Aunt Kathy's piano, which had been built around the time "Maple Leaf Rag" was a hit. The first time it was a hit. Sunlight sailed through tall, door-sized windows held together by dry, crinkled duct tape. The gray strips followed hidden cracks, at hard angles, putting the whole place in the shadow of a giant spider's web.

Lucifer, son of the morning, I'm gonna, chase you out of Earth.

The gunmen led Bremburg and me outside, across a pebbly street and into the woods. The morning gleamed. New sun lit up new dew, sweetening the brightness of the greens and yellows and dabs of purple. Birds gossiped and laughed. Critters scurried. I heard the distinct bleat of goats through the thicket to my left.

Bremburg met my eyes. His face had a coiled spring look to it. His whole body in a permanent flex. I wanted to stop our morning stroll, stand, and wait for him to exhale. There is a moment, when you're pulling back a rubber band that you realize one hair farther and the band will snap in your hands. It will sting. And you won't get to see the thing fly. Bremburg's body trembled there, at maximum tension.

The path through the woods was wide and well beaten. I heard voices up in front of us. It sounded like a party. No music or anything, but a friendly gathering. The sounds I would have expected from a group of people brought together for an old-fashioned witch trial or hanging.

The path led to a clearing. My mouth opened.

A live, animated, impressionist painting spread out before us. My eyes raced, not even focusing. They wanted too much, too fast. My original assertion that there were four men living out here in the zone collapsed under the thirty or forty people that lined the full, rich, florid garden. I saw, in one place, at one time, every color I had ever seen before.

The circular garden had a thirty-yard diameter, roughly speaking. Spirals of flowers and ground cover grew in manicured patterns. The hues were carefully juxtaposed so as not to be obnoxious — more soothing and enticing.

I could neither count nor name all the varieties of flora. Tall and short, thin and succulent, big pouty flowers and tiny puffs of petals ready to blow away with a wish. A plush grass — the kind from a putting green — wove through the arrangement.

The man walking before Bremburg and me looked back over his shoulder to see if we were suitably impressed. I'm sure my face didn't disappoint him. We were led onto a walkway made of irregular white stones. They had to have been selected with care and foresight, then placed one-by-one by hand. We tread on hundreds of hours of loving labor.

"Who's world is this," I sang out loud, but to myself. A Nas song that had come to mind.

"Whatever this is," Bremburg returned, "it's pure,"

Those gathered in the garden were as fascinating as the place itself. The men and women covered a wide spectrum of everything. I only saw one boy, in his preteens. Most of the people were between twenty and seventy. There were

Blacks and whites and Asians and Tuscarora, all in various versions of work attire. Not my kind of work. Real work. The kind that gives you callouses and uneven tans. Every person wore a form of boot, many climbing up well over the knee.

I wore sneakers rife with holes and Larry Creb's clothes that didn't quite fit. Which, when I considered it, might help me fit. Fit in.

We pushed a wave of silence before us as we walked down the aisle. The murmurs became fewer and softer with each step. The white brick path ended in the center of the clearing. The central circle had an air of the mystic about it, a post-modern altar. Four short pillars, that must have once belonged to an either an Italian restaurant or mausoleum, propped up half of a fifty-gallon drum. They'd cut it vertically, down the center, painted it white and draped it with green and violet garland. A very pretty barbecue?

They watched us. I could see a strange kind of sadness in the clean, yet unkempt faces. It triggered a new response in me, a plastic tarp over my anger and fear. Dread — heavy and stifling — pressed on my chest.

The breaths I managed were heaven. Inside the circle I drowned in the scents. A luscious, tingly, symphony of fragrances. I couldn't single one out from the mix. Nothing overpowering; nothing out of place. I drew in the deepest possible breath, trying to slowly roll the air through my nose. I heard Bremburg do the same.

This is what my wake would smell like. All the sweet flowers and rich perfumes. They did things backwards, here in the zone, laying you out before you're dead. Maybe for the best. A person should get to enjoy their own funeral.

A woman moved toward the altar-grill as we approached. Overalls and rubber boots, a red kerchief held back decades of rippling gray hair. She had no limp or strain in her gate, nor did she have any hurry. My thought being, she had no more desire than I did to reach the center of this garden.

Bremburg and I were placed before the half-drum. Our attendants placed themselves behind us. I could see now the charred grate that covered the top. The woman stood on the other side, hands clasped and pressed to her chest. Her face had the deep creases and shadows and random spots that time forces on us all. She must have had eighty years' worth. She had no hunch, though. No stoop. She stood straight and stern, as if all her bones had been replaced with fresh iron rebar.

"I'm Farrah, Foremother of this squat." A husky, firm voice.

"William Kirst, interpreter."

We waited for Bremburg. Nothing. He stared directly ahead.

"The guard's got no speaker?" Farrah asked.

I looked over at Bremburg. He held his lips together. Farrah continued to wait, narrowing her gaze, peering into his eyes. I think she knew she'd get nothing out of him. I think she might have admired his defiance.

She called him a guard. I took that to mean policeman. His badge flashed on the left strap of his empty shoulder-holster, so they had a clue.

"For more clicks than we all remember this squat's been sealed. Not a drip to the Clean. We've always ducked the guards. Monitored flow. Even from the dock, we've never had a clean to dot the squat. Till now."

Lots and lots of new meanings. I tried to ferret out some encoding while catching the speech. I wanted to divide my head and send half after the translation and put the other on alert for the details as to how and when I might die. It didn't work. I'm not that smart. If I were that smart, I would never have ended up in a garden just outside the afterlife in the first place.

Clicks. That had to be a measurement. Probably a reference to time and space.

Sealed. Drip. Flow. Although their particular meanings weren't available, they formed a lexicon.

Farrah said, "Every leak must be plugged."

That didn't sound like something I would like.

"This is a major junction." She opened up to the entire crowd. "All of the clogs valved in have a hand on the switch."

Turning my head a little to the left, I could see parts of the men standing behind me, and some of the people behind them. Amidst the ocher, vermilion, chartreuse, and violet glow of the blossoms and buds, the group grew thoughtful. They were not an angry mob. They did not seem lusty for a lynching.

Nor were they a bunch of flower girls.

"One way to plug a leak, Foremother," a man to my rear and to my right called out. He sounded pretty sure of himself.

"Do they leak?" someone else asked.

"There's risk, buddy. Any pipe can rupture. Even a clean pipe."

"So your plans?"

"Shutoff one hundred."

I rotated my head to see who petitioned for the 'shutoff one hundred' plan. I did not yet understand this creole, but that phrase did not seem to have a 'set them free' quality about it. I couldn't pick our prosecutor out of the crowd. The man directly in back of me furrowed his whole forehead at my sudden action. He stood only a foot behind me, holding his long gun near the trigger, pointed down.

I caught a glance of Bremburg as I turned back towards the altar. He looked like a gas can in the sun, soaking in the rays, getting hotter and hotter and hotter.

"A one hundred shutoff is in the box. Do we have another plan?" Farrah shouted. Her volume impressed me.

"We could drum 'em. Then they couldn't leak." This time it was a woman's voice, from directly behind me.

"And if the drum leaks?" the shut-off guy responded.

"We dot it."

"For all clicks ever?"

"We could."

"And we feed them and irrigate them for all clicks ever? Like pumping to empty rows."

A long pause set in. Too long. But it let me contemplate *rows*.

"They could work," Farrah said. "Then we wouldn't be pumping to nothing, right?"

"Yeah," some others chimed in.

"You think they won't flow?" the prosecutor asked. "Maybe not tomorrow, maybe not the next day, but someday they will duck and backwash to the Clean. Then they will leak!

"Then the guards will flow. Some of yous are too shallow to knows a click when the guard's valved into the fields. They flow in with their big-ass trackless, spitting and zapping. They fall from the sky. They gear the air, 'cause they plan we're ruptured, and they have heavy gauge gear and when they dot the apparatus. Oh, dregs. When they dot the apparatus they will clamp every clog they dot!

"And the clogs they can't clamp, they shutoff one hundred. They will light up the squat. Fire it to the ground. I dot it before, Dregs. I dot it myself. These cleans are phyllox."

The crowd didn't so much as cough once during the man's speech. Me included. His voice poured so much emotion. *Poured*. That could be part of the lexicon. The fluid, wavy, liquid lexicon. *Phyllox*? Didn't know it.

I couldn't be certain of the speech's meaning. As whole, it had been structured to persuade. I got that from tone and timing. The words were rooted in hydrodynamics. They reminded me of the plumber cants — trade language sub-lingos plumbers use when they are surrounded by their own. When they don't have to deal with carpenters, painters, and the like.

Squat. As in squatting — living somewhere you don't have the rights to occupy. This area had to be the squat. The inhabitants were squatters, though they called themselves dregs. Detritus from the bottom of a barrel.

Dot. When they dot the crop. A verb. I heard it several times now. I couldn't remember all the instances. I think one of the boys used it the night before. Dot, like *dot the i*? Like finish something correctly? Completely?

I tried to dot my own I's, to think correctly and completely, while ignoring my empty churn of a stomach. Mmmm — churn, churn the butter and then slather it on a fat golden muffin. I could see....

Dot meant *see*. The derivation wasn't clear, but it fit with the sample usage. At least, the one I could remember. I wanted my phone. I wanted records of these exchanges. I wanted a muffin and coffee and a God damn piece of electronics to round out my brainpower. I couldn't do this alone.

I wasn't alone.

Bremburg would think of something, the secret agent inspector cowboy. Surely, right now, he waited for the perfect moment to whip out his concealed machine-gun and whistle for his cruiser. It would roar in blaring sirens, throwing smoke bombs and open, to just us, its beautiful bulletproof doors.

I looked over at him again. Armed guards stood at his rear, a little to the right and left. How come he got two guards? What was I? Chopped mouthpiece?

Farrah put her arms in the air. "If there are no more plans, I say we pick a switch. White petals for drumming, red petals for shutoff one hundred. Is anyone at half?"

The only sounds came from the birds, singing to their friends and family, completely disinterested in how much longer I had on the endangered species list before being moved to 'extinct.'

"Drum the petals!"

The procession began. In single file, all of those gathered in the clearing lined up and shuffled past the white drum near the center of the white, stone circle.

Nobody looked at us. Not one.

I couldn't swallow. My throat ran so dry it hurt. My mind spun so fast I thought I might fall over.

Shutoff one hundred. This was thorny. In the context in which it had been used, it sounded like death. *Shutoff* as in *stop the flow*; *one hundred* as in *percent*.

Drum. If they were so concerned with Bremburg and I leaking their existence to the outside world, the only option, other than murdering us, would be permanent internment. Sealed up in a metaphorical drum.

Apparatus. It didn't fit. All these plumber words and they throw in a weird engineering term. *Squat* wasn't an outlier because squatters were part of general contractor lore, if not actual experience. People took up residence in abandoned or unfinished buildings. *Phyllox*, skip. Could be a brand name or highly localized slang. *Apparatus*, skip this too. Every tongue needs a word for gadget, doohickey, or thingamabob. What I had here was a lingua franca — a hybrid creole bred from other tongues and the necessity of place — gestating in isolation. I stood in a linguistic Galapagos, which would have been exciting, if not for the whole 'survival of the fittest' rule and me not adapting quickly enough.

This group survived outside of articulate civilization. Only the strong survive. Strength comes from unison. Unison comes from words.

There were three people left in line. A woman my mom's age, with a scarf over her head. She moved with no hurry and no lag, like she understood the precise amount of energy this process deserved. The two remaining men, both around seventy years old, followed her. Their eyes wet with experience, the corners feathered with wrinkles. They were in good shape, maybe from so much gardening. Their clothing scuffed and worn. Workers, all of them. People who tugged and toiled and tore.

They protected something. A thing I didn't understand, because I had no word for it.

Thing. A word with no meaning. It served as fill in, a verbal placeholder that tended to your own gapping, life-threatening ignorance.

What did they protect? It couldn't be the Zeppelin tower. You could see that for miles. That leak had flowed many clicks ago.

Two younger men opened the drum and began to count the petals. Farrah watched, trying to look unbiased.

I blamed this on Arthur Loam. And I blamed this on me. I let my spirit of adventure or vengeance or both smother what little common sense I might have had. All those stories about vigilantes swinging from roof to roof and private investigators and corporate spies and the books and comics, the games and movies ... I had actually believed that my mystery would be riddled with bullets that always missed. A matchbook from a racy club. A dropped earring. A crumpled note only I could read.

Fantasy, dressed in noir. A lethal ensemble.

My eyes dropped to the dim gun barrel near my leg. It slept. The guard had let it droop from boredom and weight.

Fiction. That's mostly what I had paid attention to in my life. Escapist, male-fantasy, grossly exaggerated, gratuitous, violent fiction. Movies, shows, comics, music. Oh the music. All the gats and AKs and pieces of respect. My musical memory threw its 50 Cent in:

You scared, you get a dog
You gully, get a gun.

"I'm gully," I mumbled.

I rammed my elbow into the stomach of the man behind me. Put my whole body into the jab. All the air shot out of him. He doubled over and the steel gun barrel came up next to me. I grabbed it with both hands and whirled to my right, using my back to force it from his hands. He fell to his knees as I continued my full turn, ending behind him. My right hand found the grip of the weapon, my left reached for my ex-guard's hair. I grabbed a clump and pressed the barrel of the gun against the back of his skull.

I shouted, "Nobody flow!"

Chapter 20

From "Tales without Interpreters"
As the brainstorming session went on, the copywriter said,
"Let me toss out this idea."
"Which one?" the art director asked.
"This one I'm about to toss out," the copywriter returned.
"There's five up there on the white board."
"Not this one."
"Because you tossed it out already?"
"I didn't toss it out yet."
"Then which one is it?" The art director's voice climbed.
"It's not any, because I haven't tossed it out yet!" the
copywriter shouted back. He uncapped a Sharpie. The
art director pulled out an X-ACTO knife. The brains
stormed.

"Kirst!" Bremburg shouted as his minders grabbed him.

Farrah held her hands up and out, palms to the crowd. She rotated her hands as if shutting invisible spigots.

I yanked my captive's hair again and pressed the barrel of the gun a wee bit harder into his skull. "Get your clamps off the guard or I spray this dreg's bucket!"

Farrah looked at the men holding Bremburg. "Turn him. It's solid," she said.

They looked at each other, then at her, then let Bremburg go. My heart thumped so hard everybody could hear it. They'd rush me any second. They knew my myocardial infarction was seconds away. Bremburg looked around, more amazed than anybody. I expected him to spin into action, punch, kick, grab a gun. He didn't seem interested.

"Farrah," I announced. "The guard and I are going to spill." I tugged my hostage's hair. "This dreg is with us till the gate. Are you at half?"

"Your speaker?" she asked. "Your speaker's like a dreg. But you're a clean?"

"I'm a dreg and a clean."

"You don't click," she said.

"Are you at half or do I shutoff one hundred this dreg?"

"We can't risk a leak. You can't spill."

I raised the clump of hair in my hand, bringing the man to his feet. The gun stayed tight to his head.

"We won't leak. We flow and never backwash." I started walked backward, down the path. "This was all an accident."

Bremburg looked me in the eye, steady as a statue. It made me nervous. I thought I had the situation well — and literally — in hand. He didn't share my opinion.

"Kirst," he said, "confess the tracker and the backup."

I nodded. "He's a guard." I looked around to everyone. I had their attention. "If he doesn't backwash, the guards will valve on. They'll flow from the sky. Hundreds of guards."

Some of the locals looked at each other. They didn't know that we had pulled the tracking transmitter in the cruiser or that the cops would never ever think to look for us here. My threat must have sounded plausible.

Bremburg still didn't move. He watched the space behind me, saying nothing. I stopped backing up near the end of the path. Something cold and metallic pressed against my head.

"They'll flow from the sky and in the trackless." I forced a passable snarl into my voice. "Hundreds of guards with serious gear."

Farrah locked her eyes to mine. My heart thundered. My face burned from the flush. Through my hair and scalp and bone, I could tell a handgun dented my flesh. Birds sang above my taxed cardiovascular system. Everyone else stayed hushed, waiting for the Foremother's decree.

"They will spill!" the man who wanted us dead shouted. "Shut 'em down!"

A swell of approval ground through the crowd. We hadn't looked like trouble before, now we did. I made things worse.

The guy behind me pressed his weapon harder against my head.

"I … I, hold up," I yelled. What did these people understand? Plumbers, builders, gardeners— "Not my job!"

The quake in the crowd fell still.

"Not my job!" I barked again. "It's not our job to spill. We came to dot the Zeppelin spike. That's all. No more. Dotting the squat is not my job and it's not the guard's job."

The murmuring started again. People glanced at each other. The Foremother gave me a look that said, basically, "Hadn't thought of that."

"Bury the pipe, Trent," she said, directing it over my shoulder.

The piece of metal departed from my skull. Grumbles rose from the crowd. They were not happy, nor did they seem unhappy.

She said to the group, "The cleans can flow the squat."

The crowd became loud. A sense of relief tossed about with the displeasure.

The man I held spun and grabbed the shotgun. I let go of both his hair and the weapon. He brought the barrel up to my nose, crushing his teeth against themselves, eyes wet red.

"No, Steph." Farrah remained calm. "The clean, his speaker's like a dreg. Ear it?"

Steph backed off two inches. The end of the barrel had a hole so deep and black and final. I gazed into the second one in two days. Twice is not enough to make one used to it.

"Not a drip, Steph." I tried sincerity. I'm usually good at it. "I'm solid."

He didn't seem convinced. I realized taking his weapon was not something he would take lightly. I had committed a life-threatening faux pas. His finger slithered on the trigger.

Farrah fluttered down from the altar. An angel in overalls. "Ear it up," she said as she marched. "My hand is on the switch." She blew in next to Steph, brushing him as she passed him. She took my hand and kept going, tugging me along behind her. She held up our hands and said, "My hand."

"Mother!" Somone's protest poked above the crowd noise. "They will leak. They will. There is no ever after."

"There is," Farrah called back over her shoulder as she walked us back down the path. "In death."

Chapter 21

From "Tales without Interpreters"
This recently successful movie director sits down before a new hair stylist of the type he can just now afford. He shakes his billowing mane and, as he is a director, yelps a few orders. He settles back, fully expecting them to be carried out with precision. First comes the highly relaxing shampoo. So relaxing in fact, that he drifts near sleep. A few moments later he is awakened by gentle tugging on the back of his head. He parts his eyelids and looks in the mirror. The stylist has his massive sheaf of hair pulled back, scissors open and poised a quarter inch from his scalp. "Cut!" he cries, ... and so she does.

As Farrah led me by the hand down a thin path, I turned to wave Bremburg along. He looked on either side. No one moved to stop him, so he started off behind us. The path went through a patch of trees so layered and bent, my sense of direction gave up. Quit, amidst the green flittering viridian, emerald, olive, teal....

"So, my..." as if I'd never spoken before. "You plan to shut us off one hundred?"

"We ain't killers," Farrah returned. Then, in a fairly straight English dialect, "Not me and none of them. We ain't exactly good 'n plenty, but we ain't rat poison neither."

I looked back at Bremburg. "We have evaded a death sentence. This group has got a record, but no homicides."

"You've dropped the lingo," I said to Farrah.

"Glad I remember how," she said. "Haven't spoken regular in twenty-five years. How'm I doing?"

"Quite nicely," I said.

A pleasant little house sat in a glen cut out of the thick woods. Flowers lined the two sides I could see from our angle of approach. Blue shutters hung by the windows. Gray bars covered the glass. She led us around to the back patio, a slab of concrete jutting out from under the house. There was no backyard. There were rows and rows of grape vines, extending in patches that made best use of the rolling terrain. Bright green, dark green remnants, stitched together into a lush comforter. A set of mismatched aluminum furniture faced the bending shapes.

"Have seats." Farrah motioned to the chairs.

"Please," I said. "After you?"

Bremburg passed me. "What's the twenty?" he asked in a nearly sub-audible grumble.

"Running intel now," I whispered back.

Farrah took the chair and sat looking off into the fields. "I'd offer you something, but it's the help's day off."

"We're fine," I lied, picking a seat next to her. Bremburg stood, eyes sweeping the scene.

"You picked up our lingo pretty quick," Farrah said. "You speak some of the contractor 'gots?'"

"I can't afford not to," I answered. "You want for me to pay an interpreter on top of what those guys charge to drop in a toilet?"

She smiled, sat back, stretched her arms, then pointed to Bremburg. "Your friend is not big on relaxing."

"He's a cop," I said. "This is how he relaxes — looking for the next crime."

"Well I best send you off before he catches sight of one."

"It's that easy?" I asked.

"Let's just say, we don't seek any tourism business."

"So that's it? You're going to let us go? Not everyone in the group seemed to think that was the solution."

"Pooosh." Farrah flicked her wrist, as if flinging something behind her. "They were looking for an excuse to let yous go. Lucky for all of us you gave 'em one. You confused the Hell out of them talking like you're of us. Like you belong."

"Like you belong," I said. "That's why you don't talk regular no more."

Farrah smiled again. "Not much call for it."

"A shame," I said. "You speak English well."

"My daddy always insisted on it. No jargon in the house," Farrah said. "The good ol' days, huh?"

"I don't know. I wouldn't have a job back then." I tried to get Bremburg to sit by looking at him, but we hadn't been married long enough for that to work. He gave me a twitch of a scowl and continued his landscape study.

"What yous all doing here?" Farrah asked.

I tried to conjure up a sympathetic look on my face. "It's got nothing to do with you. We didn't even know you were here. We thought the Zone was pretty much deserted."

"That is not a fulfilling answer."

"We wanted to see the spike. To give you any more than that, I'd have to lie."

Farrah smirked.

"How about you?" I inquired. "What are you doing here?"

"I stopped by some time ago," Farrah said. "Back when there were a few Tuscarora groups still living here."

"So you are not Tuscarora?"

"I do not have that honor. I happened upon the Reservation, as opposed to being raised on it. I liked the place, so I stayed. We worked out an arrangement whereby it was worth them letting me."

"You said 'were' Tuscarora. So there aren't any groups here now?"

"A few individuals," Farrah answered. "No families. They've spread out and over the country now. The only thing holding them together was customs and language. Kids didn't practice the customs. Once the language stopped being used, they all went their separate ways. The accountants went to live near other accountants, the medicals near the other meds. Two generations it took. That was all. Two and out. When I got here, the place looked like a retirement community. Those ones what welcomed me — they all feeding the begonias now."

"Oh," I let out. I glanced at Bremburg. He stopped his observation of the scene to meet my eyes. I think he might have wanted a translation of Farrah's tale. I didn't want to slow her down, so I returned my attention to her.

"This community." I remained confused. "What—"

"Misfits like me," Farrah cut me off. "Either they drifted by and stuck, like seeds on the wind — or I sought them out, like seeds from the feed store. Either way, those what lingered got a lesson from me. I taught them our argot for here on the Rez or anywhere in the Zone. Those Tuscarora taught me well. A family's got to communicate. I didn't forget my daddy, neither. Anyone living here had to learn the lingo. I didn't go for English, for reasons I don't need to tell you."

"The mother tongue is a tough one," I said.

"Truth on truth," Farrah said.

"You developed your own argot?"

"That makes it sound so smart, like I planned out all the nouns and vowels. The 'got grew much as these gardens. Transplants, tending and not nearly enough weeding."

"It's fascinating," I said. "I noticed a good deal of plumber lingo in the lexicon. Allusions to pipes, containers, water based—"

Farrah's hand stopped me. Her face said I hadn't done the reading last night or asked her how much she weighed. "It might be best if you all made your way now."

"I'm sorry," I said "I didn't mean to, ah … do whatever it is I just did."

"I said you all wouldn't be leaking." Farah put her hands on the arms of the chair and pushed herself up. "So, let's not prick a hole."

I looked to Bremburg. "Time to roll."

"Roger that," he returned.

"Let me get you to the road." Farrah walked off the patio and rounded the house.

"I talk a lot," I followed a few steps behind. "But not about you. All of you. The community."

"I know," she said as we walked. "It ain't you, it's them. They've been skittish ever since the spike got fixed."

"The Zeppelin pier?"

"It's like a beacon. We don't like beacons."

"Because you shouldn't be living here," I answered no one's question but my own. Bremburg looked at me again.

I guessed he guessed the gist of our conversation. "Are you worried about oversight?"

"Nobody wants to oversee this place."

"I mean, like a view from above."

"No." We reached the end of her driveway. "That LTA tower is of no one's mind. Not ours and especially not yours. I don't know why you wanted to see it so badly, but you did and now you can go. I hope it was a satisfying visit."

"Who—"

She shook her head, looking up into the sky for a moment. Then returned her attentions to us. "Listen," she restarted. "These people found some peace out here. Peace that none of us found out in the world." Farrah looked at Bremburg. "They used to call you officers of the peace. Protectors of the peace. I have a hunk of hope that's still true." Farrah pointed to her left, down the gray and green crumble of a used-to-be street. "Your car is a mile or so in that direction. While I've enjoyed our exchanges, I'm hoping I never see you two again."

"Yes," I said.

Bremburg nodded. We started off.

"Please," Farrah said to our backs. "Keep your mouth shut."

Yeah, I thought. Not my specialty.

Chapter 22

From "Hoe of Babylon"
Canisius University has added Ecumenical Finance
Law to this year's syllabus. The dean of the facilitation
department "Prayed the course would be profitable
without getting the school into any trouble."

We found the police cruiser as we left it. No slashed tires
or broken windows. Our phones sunned themselves on
the front windshield, next to Bremburg's pistol. Our lovely
phones. How beautiful they looked on their little vacations.
My chrome cylinder was too hot to touch. Bremburg picked
up his bendable flat black piece of carbon fiber with two
fingers, opened the car door, and tossed it on the dash. I
blew on mine, rolling it on my hands. Bremburg shoved his
sidearm into his shoulder holster with the look of a parent
catching up to an errant child at a grocery store. I half
expected him to say, "and stay there." He flopped into the
car.

"That went well," I said as I got in.

Bremburg turned to me, eyes partly closed. "You ever
discharge a weapon?"

"Nope."

"Shouldn't handle 'em then."

"I think I executed fine."

"Handles are grip-keyed, Kirst." He held his palm up to
me. "Unless your prints were filed in, you never could have
discharged that twenty gauge."

"Oh." You learn something new every day. Farrah had
said "it's solid" and her men had put their guns down. She'd
known that I couldn't have fire that weapon.

"You're lucky you can talk," he said.

I didn't know how to take that.

Detective Bremburg took his phone off the dash and gave it a squeeze. It went limp and he placed it on his shoulder like a radio. It stiffened and clutched him like an eagle's talon.

"Ethel, Open channel, Dispatch," he said.

We sat through a pause, listening.

"Dispatch to Bremburg, go," came through the car.

"I-C-S-two-fourteen."

"Copy that."

"O-O-S, admin. Copy?"

"Copy."

"End," he said. "Ethel out."

"Ethel?" I couldn't help but ask. "Is that your phone's handle?"

"It's a name you don't hear on the street."

"What if it catches on? What if it's the next big baby name?" He was right to ignore me. If you're picking a word with which to wake up your phone, Ethel seemed pretty safe. I didn't have an activation word for mine. In my line of work, you never knew what kind of lexeme might come up. Any combination of sounds could ring out at any time. I relied on touch.

I held my phone to my face, exhaled on it, and rubbed the mist off the chrome and onto my shirt. I rubbed the phone between my hands. Held it up. Checked for scratches, battery life and, finally, messages.

There were none. I left like I'd been around the world, when, in fact, I'd been up in Niagara County for about nine hours, most of which I would've slept right through had I been home.

I couldn't go home. I'd tried that two nights ago and almost got killed. I'd been in so much shit these last few hours, I almost forgotten how much shit I was in back home.

We shot down the road too fast, even for a cop car. It took years to get back to the main road. When we did, we exhaled at the same time. Paved roads, other cars, signs and markers and advanced civilization.

"So," I started. "As far as intel goes … we got some, right?"

"This case keeps opening and opening and opening," Bremburg returned.

"Like one of those presents your mom gives you in a huge box, with a smaller one inside, then inside that is a smaller one and then another smaller box—"

"Yeah," he cut me off. "Just like."

We rode for a little while in silence. Not my preferred way to travel. I could understand the man needing a little peace; though, I hoped he didn't need too much.

"What's the angle?" Bremburg asked, staring out at the black and gray highway.

I didn't understand the question and my lack of understanding had nothing to do with translation. The words worked just fine, all three of them. More would have helped. Beggars can't be chewers if they don't have enough to gnaw on.

"Whose angle?" I asked. "Farrah's? Mine? Whomever rehabbed the Zeppelin tower?"

Bremburg glanced at me. "Whose you got?"

"I got nothing," I said.

"You tipped me off to the tower. You lead me to believe it might be cogent to the investigation."

"I didn't know that," I said. "I just passed along a tip."

"Still not seeing the connection. Thought I might after the recon. Now it's all a big negative."

"Not as big as finding squatters. The Quarantine Zone was supposed to be empty. Those people were not authorized to occupy that land. That's another big negative. We now have a double negative. In my world, that's a positive."

"I want to push you out of my car."

"You are justified," I said. "You could point your firearm at me but that hasn't worked for anyone else who's tried lately, partner."

"Not your partner."

"Positive," I returned. "A positive from the two negatives. Two wrongs make a right."

"Two wrongs lengthen a sentence and diminish prospects for parole."

"There is a connection," I said. "There has to be a link between the squatters, the Zeppelin spike, Paul Dombrowski's murder, and—"

I stopped. I was forbidden from saying it out loud.

"Arthur Loam." Bremburg completed the sentence for me.

I neither confirmed nor denied his addition.

"That's four wrongs," Bremburg said. "What's that in your world?"

"That is a soon-to-be-out of work mouthpiece."

We drove down the Thruway, hungry, thirsty, tired and, for me anyway, confounded.

———<>———

Bremburg did not dwell in a newer development, the kind that catered to a specific vocation. He had an upper in a duplex in north Beau Fleuve. You could tell by the silent smiles and nods, friendly waves from the brightly painted porches and across tiny, edged lawns that this was an old neighborhood where people still mixed. We passed a dozen people as we rolled down the street and slid into the spot in front of Bremburg's house. People, in the late morning. The word *Saturday* rose in the vast night sky of my memory, eclipsing my sense of time.

"Saturday," I said out loud. "It's got a nice ring to it."

"It's also today." Bremburg paused. "I think."

Once inside he pointed to his shower, to which I took no offence. The blistering water felt like love. I washed three times, each pass removing a new, deeper layer of grime and salt and the chemicals my body had oozed under duress. The steam invaded and freed my sinuses, tripling the blood flow in my brain. I got smarter.

It is not unusual for people to have their best ideas in a shower. The solitude, the soothing distraction, the fact that no one else is talking to, at, or around you. Most people are at their best when no one's speaking. I don't care for what that says about me and my profession.

This particular shower gave me an idea about showers. Water, anyway. Fresh water. The squatters used a pidgin argot based on a plumber's lexicon. A whole colony of plumbers made no sense. The plumber trade was a support function. Everyone needed one. Maybe two. Not forty or fifty. You didn't need that many unless the function was not support — unless plumbing was central to function of the group.

I rinsed, wrapped a towel around my middle and grabbed my phone. What was that word? The one that didn't fit with pipes. And buckets, drips, clogs … *phyllox*. I fanned out my phone and tried a search. Phylloxera was as close as I got. Phyllox to phylloxera might be a natural shortening of the word, like bus from omnibus, or piano from piano forte, so I pressed on to grape phylloxera, an insect that feeds on roots of the Vitis vinifera grape, eventually killing the plants. I dove deeper into my phone. The Vitis vinifera grape was of course, one of the most common wine grapes in the world.

While I had gotten smarter, Bremburg had laid out cloths for me and cooked eggs. In butter. The scent threw my massive hunger switch.

At the table, I sat like a little brother in bad hand-me-downs. Shorts with big pockets and a Police Athletic League T-shirt. At that point, I had worn three men's clothes in two days, beating my old record by two. We sat across from each other at his tiny kitchen table. The midmorning sun sifted through sheers on the double-hung window over his sink. It all felt very quaint.

"I have a hunch about the squatters," I blurted out, trying to keep my toast from coming out of my mouth with the words.

Bremburg chewed. He didn't seem to think I needed any encouragement in order to go on.

"Right," I said. "They called us 'phyllox.'"

"I noted it. I've been called many things in my career, never that."

"It's an aphid that destroys grape vines," I replied. "It was a metaphor."

Bremburg stabbed another clump of scrambled eggs. "Is that dangerous?"

"Possibly," I said. "But in this case, it's a stand-in word for two guys about to shut down their racket."

"What racket?"

"Wine," I said. "They're making wine in the Quarantine Zone."

"Other than their presence, that's not illegal. Hell, I don't blame them. Hope they got a still, too." Bremburg ate and gazed into the light from the window. I ate and stared, too.

"Handcuffs are not just two bracelets," Bremburg said. "There's got to be a couple of links between them."

Yes, I thought. This ladder's got more than one rung. The path over the pond has many stones. I needed a layover in Chicago before I could fly on to Vegas. I unfurled the screen on phone and brought up my file on Arthur Loam. That link I could not talk about. You know when you misplace your sunglasses and you look all over the living room, then the kitchen, your bedroom, the kitchen — who knows why — and then you end up back in the living room and they're glaring at you? I wanted my search of Loam's files to be like that. Maybe something shady would glare at me.

It didn't happen. Bremburg cleaned up the breakfast dishes, went for his own shower and I consumed more coffee and more data, generating more and more frustration. It will not end here, I commanded myself. I will go to my grave — no, to burial grounds. That asshole had the gall to correct me. Not internment, but burial grounds. As in sacred. As in Native American. The only ones who would have ... what did Isla call it?

Standing. That's what she told her client about his lawsuit. He didn't have standing. The court would not recognize his concerns. A player had to have skin the game, a dog in that hunt. My whole mess started because Loam had a stake in the game. And Paul Dombrowski must have been holding it.

I brought up my file on Paul Dombrowski. Age sixty-four, owner of a small vineyard outside of Lockport. Twenty miles from the Quarantine Zone. He raised money for cancer research because his husband, aged thirty, died too young. Alex Lightwood. I ran his name next, knowing what I would find. He had been a proud member of the Tuscarora Nation.

That seemed about right.

One of the reasons an interpreter takes a job at a firm when they are fresh out of school is the difficulty in starting from nothing. Drumming up business is like being locked in a lightless cooler, tapping on the walls, feeling for a crack in the economy. Hooting and hollering, hoping someone hears you, while you sit on a drum in the dark. Yes, you've got to have some skill. Ultimately, it's who you know. Connections.

Bremburg walked into the kitchen wearing clean, comfy clothes, hair still gleaming from the wet. Two heads are, sometimes — not all the time, like if you're flipping a coin or trying to put on a crewneck sweater — better than one. He could help.

"What's next?" he asked.

Maybe even more heads, I thought.

"We throw a party."

Chapter 23

From "Tales without Interpreters"
The CEO examined the report from his head of security,
nodded and said, "Execute the program." The ex-military
security specialist was not in the habit of questioning
orders. He had expected questions about budget, scope or
timing. He never imagined being told to kill the program
everyone agreed they needed. He followed orders,
nonetheless. Eight months later, their company lost four
million dollars in re-routed transactions from a fully
preventable hack.

Larry and Ann arrived first. They brought beer. Chapman
Sadabahar, my client from the drayage company, arrived
next. He brought a bottle of white wine. The three sat in
Bremburg's small living room, giving each other the occasional eyebrow pop of people with proximity as their only
thing in common. Bremburg joined them after a couple of
minutes, adding nothing.

The doorbell rang and I answered it with Bremburg
stood close behind me.

"This better be life-threatening," Isla said as she entered.

"What can I get you?" Bremburg asked, very nearly smiling.

"Gin and tonic," I said.

"I wasn't—" Bremburg said.

"It's for me." She pumped a quick smile with just the
outer corners of her mouth. "Nice to meet you."

I ushered Isla into the living room and introduced
her with a wave. She sat down in a well-worn recliner. I
remained in the doorway, knowing the chime would sound
again. Five fully extended minutes later it did.

"Hi, uh...." B Carlisle was just short enough to see under my arm, down the little hall to the gathering. Hearing their words held up by surprise made me smile for real.

"I very glad you could join us." I backed against the wall to let them in.

"This seems more like a cocktail party than a quick chat about the other night." They didn't move.

"Why can't it be both?"

"I'm dressed for the later, not the former." They wore their trapse-around-the-concrete-jungle outfit.

"You get nothing but empathy from me," I said. "I'm wearing someone else's clothes entirely. I don't even fit in when I'm alone in a room."

B Carlisle entered the house and walked down to the living room. Bremburg introduced them to everyone. I followed as far and the doorway and stopped.

"Proceed, Will." Bremburg ordered from the bar in the corner.

"Thank you all for coming," I said as they situated themselves.

"Kind of an if-then," Larry said, smirking. He realized no one else laughed and lost his grin.

"Officer Bremburg wants to question you all, query, cross-examine, perform his due diligence. Let me emphasize, stress, underline, make that redundant. Police Officer Bremburg has questions, queries, information requests, will cross examine."

"As in, not you," Isla realized.

"Precisely." At least the lawyer present could, at some later date, reasonably testify to the fact that I wasn't staging this show. The instinct to protect my license still ran through me.

"Officer Bremburg?" I motioned to him.

"Why is Arthur Loam holding a spike in the Niagara County Quarantine Zone?"

To Isla, I said, "The party of the first part, Loam, Arthur, has acquired a Zeppelin stand in fringe property. The motivation is in question."

Isla supplied the expected perplexed-to-annoyance look and said, "I have nothing to offer."

To Chapman, I said, "Arthur Loam has leased a tower in a no-go. What's his tack?"

"I can't see the alignment," Chapman added.

"Larry and Ann," I said. "Loam added on Zeppelin landing hardware in fried real space. Query expected output?"

Larry shrugged as I looked at Ann, who sipped her beer, and grinned beyond what I thought appropriate for the situation.

"Ann?" I asked?

"Will?"

"You're clever."

"You're sweet," she said. "Neither trait is going assist in this inquest. Not enough data."

B Carlisle observed everything from the back wall.

"How is this relevant?" Isla asked.

"That remains in question," I answered. "We are on a fishing expedition."

While I never liked being trite, I loved that idiom. It saved me time and breath. There's nothing like a good ol' wives' tale, old saying, or sports analogy to bring people together.

"What's the haul?" Chapman announced. "No one gets anywhere on an empty belly."

"Or," Ann said. "What's the pathology? This tower is either a malignancy or a cure."

"Pardon me?" Bremburg looked at me.

"The spike's job is unclear," I said. "Is it there to rehabilitate or prevent. A tip as to which might give us a clue as to motive."

Bremburg smirked and nodded. Ann hadn't given him an answer, but his eyes pointed hard at something I couldn't see. An idea or an image in his mind.

"A parameter has changed," Larry said. "The Zone ran stable for years. Then this user adds on some seemingly useless peripheral, for what? Every user wants to maintain stability even as they add on functionality, so a parameter has changed."

"Or will change," Ann added. "The hardware could be prophylactic."

"Ah." I pressed my hands to face, steepling my fingers around my nose. The germinated seed of an idea had flown into my brain. It tried to break its shell and root and sprout.

"Something new," I nodded at Larry. "Might be coming to the Zone," I nodded at Ann. "That will create a market for lighter-than-air transportation." I bowed to Chapman. I lifted my head and turned to Bremburg. He leaned back against the wall, hanging a cold beer by the neck. He shook his stooped head.

"Laws?" B Carlisle asked the room. "There is a special session of the legislature right now."

"Sounds like a law," Isla added. "Every time I've witnessed developers acquiring land with abandon, it was due to an impending change in zoning regulations or code. This tower reminds me of that. An undesirable property becoming desirable — laws do that."

"Any on your docket?" I asked.

"Not my kind of law," she replied. "You need to conference with a political."

"Oh." I gulped.

I just remembered something I'd forgotten to do. I took out my phone. One of my friends was not at this party. In the last three days I had been chased by car and on foot, had both long and short firearms aimed at me with intent to kill, spent the night in an oven, and been subjected to a trial that almost left me serving a beautiful garden as a wind chime. In this time, I had not thought to call—

"Marin?"

"Will?"

"How are you?" I winced at my own lame question. I hadn't spoken to Marin since I'd abandoned her at Rigoletto's in front of Dombrowski's dead body.

"Now you care? Three days after an impromptu dismissal — on the street no less — and now you care?"

"I'm ... it will take too long to explain. Listen—"

"Take too long? What? Am I, like, on retainer? You can only put in so many dating hours and your docket's filled?"

"Listen," I said. "What do you know about the Niagara County Quarantine Zone?"

"Pardon me? Is that some interpreter term for 'I'm sorry'?"

"The QZ, Marin. Is there any legislation pending appending the parameters of the NCQZ?"

"I have no comment at this time."

"This is weighty. Really. I would not caucus with you if this wasn't a capital issue."

"Really? You wouldn't caucus with me because you liked to? Because I was fun or interesting?"

"I'm—"

"The jury's out on what you are."

The dead air made me wish I flicked the screen open for a video chat. Was Marin rolling her eyes? Puffing her cheeks? Gnashing her teeth?

After what must have been twelve hours, she said, "I'll call you back in five." Click.

"An ex?" Ann leaned in the doorway, arms crossed in the smug style they teach you in Mom school.

"Very."

"I would've prescribed heavier groveling."

"It's an emergency."

"Then you grasp your grovel bag and squeeze it hard."

A woman's voice whispered throughout the house, "There are two adult humans at the front door."

Bremburg brushed past me. "You haul anyone else in?"

"Negative," I replied. "We're full up."

Bremburg opened the door and stepped back.

"We could wait no longer for an invitation," a man said as he, and a woman, both in dark suits, walked in from hallway. Bremburg walked backward, until he pressed himself against the wall, mouth open in an I-can't-believe-this fashion.

"Evening," the woman said.

"Evening," Bremburg said.

Without touching us, they moved Ann and I back into the living room with the others, and took a good, slow look at each of us.

"Sorry to interpose," the man said. "I am Special Agent Danh and this is Special Agent McClellan of the FBI. And we were wondering, What's the occasion?"

Chapter 24

From "Tales without Interpreters"
"If you want to help," the wife said, half out the door. "Can 'em." She pointed to a bushel of fresh peppers, kissed her husband goodbye, and left. The husband, a newly retired railroad worker, had promised to help out around the house. He had no idea what might be wrong with the peppers. They looked like they would work, like they were ready for the mason jars his wife had boiled up yesterday. As she'd been running the household for forty years, he wasn't going to start questioning her now. He took the bushel out to the compost pile and got rid of them like she'd asked.

Danh and McClellan were fit and fashionable; their confident stances, darting eyes, thinly disguised relaxation all pegged them as law enforcement and a little on the elite side. Even if they hadn't said it, I would have guessed FBI. They were both the same height, which made McClellan seem tall. That or the grave blue suit. It had power sewn into the seams. Trim, but not restrictive. Short, oaken hair. Fair skin. I couldn't decide if she was attractive. With Danh, I made up my mind quickly. He had a smile so fake I don't even know why he bothered.

"What can I get you?" Bremburg joined us in the living room.

"Just some answers, thank you very much," Danh replied.

"For that I'll need some questions, partner," Bremburg said.

"The motivation behind congregating here?"

"Social," Bremburg said. "Next?"

"You." Danh pointed to Ann. "You associated with Arthur Loam?"

"If you could restart—"

"No statements," Isla shouted.

Bremburg put his arm out. "She's unaffiliated."

"You the lady's mouthpiece?" Danh sneered.

"This ain't nothing but a party," Bremburg returned.

"I do not observe any snacks or music."

"It's a book club."

Danh chuckled.

Bremburg did not. "I invited you in as a professional courtesy."

B Carlisle slid clear, narrow glasses onto their face with the slow arch of a nature photographer. Danh watched them. He stood like rebar in a suit. Fists on hips, pushing back the jacket because actually taking off his shirt and flexing would be too much. He moved his gaze from person to person, meeting everyone's eyes, ending with me. Locking me down with a stare, he said "Mac?"

"A...." I had no solid response. "No?"

Agent McClellan took out her phone — a half-moon so black it made my eyes cold — and read out loud, "Ann Crep. Lawrence Crep. Isla Vokevitch. Chapman Sadabahar. B Carlisle. William Kirst."

"B Carlisle," Danh said through his dead smile, "we are exercising our personal image rights at this time."

"Noted," they replied, glasses aimed at the authorities.

Danh took a position in front of me close enough to hurt. "Ah, Mr. Kirst. Enjoying your social congregating?"

"Not so much anymore."

"My apologies."

"Your apologies what? What do they do?"

"I ... for...." His face scrunched a little. I love when they do that.

"Apologies to me?" I found his eyes. "Are you supplying apologies to me for something you've perpetrated?"

"There's no perpetrating. I'm executing my duties," rolled out of his mouth.

"Then apologies are out of order, are they not? Who apologizes for serving the public good?"

Danh opened his mouth, closed it, then opened it again. "Mac?"

Agent McClellan continued to read. "Crep, Lawrence, clearance level C-O-N-fourteen."

"Maybe you can translate this question for your friend." Danh kept looking me in the eyes. "Can you continue to function in your current capacity under suspension of federal security clearance?"

"Larry—"

"I got it." He cut me off.

"Sadabahar, Chapman," McClellan announced, "Bonded."

"Oh." Danh pursed his lips. "That sounds important."

"Vokevitch, Beverly, license to practice law, subject to review."

"What?" Isla shot up. "On what grounds? Threatening actions are impermissible."

They ignored her.

"Kirst, William," McClellan went on. "License to facilitate, subject to review."

"Again," Isla spat, "Grounds? I formally object to any actions under threat. This is a flagrant misapplication of duties."

"Not sure what you are saying," Danh kind of sang. "But it is not relevant. We can still get temporaries on all you."

"Ahem," Anne coughed.

"Crep, Ann." McClellan poked her phone twice. She looked up. "Nothing."

"Wha hoo." Ann waved her hands. "I'm clean. No restraints. I can practice whatever I want to practice."

"No one's above the law," Danh said.

"You got nothing," Ann replied.

B Carlisle did not make a sound. I thought they might be trying to hide, standing up in a room that just barely fit all of us. Then I thought something else.

"What about Carlisle?" I asked.

"They didn't bother," B Carlisle said. "They think they can buy me off. A favor somewhere in the future. A scoop. Some data. They think I'm cheap."

"Is that your price, B?" I looked at McClellan. "A scoop?"

B Carlisle replied, "If you have to ask, you can't afford it."

"What's the beef, Danh?" Bremburg asked. "What are you trying to dig up by harassing my associates?"

"Dispersal," he said. "We want everyone to vacate the premises."

"Enjoinment is beyond your jurisdiction," Isla said.

"Have you not been listening, lady?" Danh motioned to me. "Kirst, you want to engage? Back the lady up? Why don't you lay out the deal to all your associates. We will agitate the lifestyle of anyone who fails to the vacate the premises in five minutes."

Tone, body language, the bulk of basic words — my friends understood the sentence just fine. As little interest as I had in all the nonverbal parts of my training, the effect could not be belittled. The real reason interpreters exist is not to translate words, it's to help people get together. There are very few meetings that couldn't be conducted with decent software tuned to the parties involved. Most meetings could be conducted by video, with parties thousands of miles apart. Still, humans like to get into each other's space, watch each other's hands flutter, eyes roll or smile and nod. They spend billions of dollars and millions of hours traveling for the privilege, dragging people like me along because sometimes *fine* means *exquisite* and sometimes it's followed by a huff and a chin pressed tight to the chest and means the exact opposite.

Danh chose to visit a group of people for the purpose of intimidation. He had no real authority here, so he chose to use posture and base words to scare my friends at my party. Fine.

You don't mess with my clan.

I turned and put myself between Special Agent Danh and the rest of the room. "Larry, I think these are the users that hacked me two nights ago. They accessed data on my circles. But every handshake is send and receive, am I right?

"You are right," Larry returned.

"Four minutes, Mr. Kirst," Danh said.

"Give and take," I said. "Puts and gets, in and out. Life is a two-way street." I thought that covered everybody. "Isla, establish a front five-oh-one. Incorporate in New York State."

Isla got quizzical, scrunching up her eyes, then tapping her chin. Finally, she let out a thin smile. "I'd be happy to." She took out her phone.

"Chapman" I continued. "We'll need an open account — let's call it Book Club Limited — and seed a positive balance of ... I don't know ... what can you shuttle?"

"A quarter million dollars is easy to move and looks pretty bad."

"Bull," I said. "Larry, toggle on full permissions for Special Agent Danh. Make sure he's got complete access to the source fund account."

"Easily executable," Larry replied. He also took out his phone.

Dahn scowled. He looked at his partner, who had obviously boarded the wrong bus. She had no idea where this was going but didn't want to show it. I knew my way around confusion, though. You can't hide those arching eyebrows from me.

"Whoa," Danh said to me. "What's this account access?"

"I am establishing your personal access to our book club's funds." I watched my friends tap, tap, tap away on their phones.

Danh asked, "Are you attempting to bribe a federal officer?"

"Negative." I turned to face the agent. "We're going to frame it to look like you already took one. Ann, I hope you're not feeling excluded."

"A little."

"Carlisle," I said. "I haven't done this in a while, but how's 'FBI shakes down local book club' for a headline?"

"I might go bigger," they replied. "Like, 'FBI corruption scheme uncovered.'"

"You don't want to start this." McClellan's voice rose.

"I didn't." My voice stayed flat.

"Hey, mouthpiece," Danh cut in, "You can't stare down the FBI."

"I would appear that's what I'm—" My phone tickled. Probably Marin calling back. "Hold your position."

"I got something for you to hold," Dahn said.

"Hey." Bremburg put himself in the middle of the room. "Now how 'bout that drink I offered?"

Danh stared at me. Calculating, I imagine. McClellan's lower jaw stuck out. Bremburg opened his arms and bowed his head a tad. I said hello to Marin, but I listened to Bremburg.

"You got an operation going," he said. "I don't warrant a brief. That's okay. We are all working the same side here. My hunch is you all have been surveilling Loam as he might be rolled up. Whatever we're running might deep-six your operation. Am I close?"

"We are not at liberty to divulge," Danh said.

"Nope." Bremburg nodded. "You stick to protocol."

"You need to cease and desist."

"Not sure we can comply at this time."

"We are here to see that you do."

"In my house?" Bremburg's arms curled. He pointed to the floor. "You gonna bring that shit into my house?"

The two men squared off, chests out, neither prepared to back down for reasons that escaped cases and criminals. I've seen a lot of meetings devolve from purpose to personal. It is never progress. I needed to take control of the meeting, make sure this didn't get physical.

Through the phone, Marin said, "nuclear," and everything stopped, as if a tiny bomb kicked up a mushroom cloud in my head. I lowered my phone.

"How about arresting Arthur Loam?" I tossed into the room. "Does that help anyone out?"

Chapter 25

From "Tales without Interpreters"
The DEA agent knew using a civilian as an undercover
operative could be dangerous, but the botanist had
already been approached by the drug dealers. They were
inviting him into their circle. The best possible scenario …
so long as the agent was careful. She took every possible
precaution, even requisitioning a high-gain collector — a
sensitive listening device, and an audio rifle — a narrow-
beam sound projector that let her speak to the botanist
without anyone else hearing. It all almost came in handy
when she intercepted a message sent to the botanist's
contact. The drug dealer's car door opened. The botanist
went to get in. "Your cover is blown!" the agent shouted
through her audio rifle. The botanist heard her and smiled,
thinking 'Blown. In full bloom. How nice. Everything must
be perfect.' No one ever saw him again.

Bremburg had an ancient porch. Not that it looked old
or decrepit, more vestigial. As if one could sit outside on
a summer's night and talk to the neighbors, disembogued
from the air-conditioned wombs, severed from the monitors,
masks, and mics. I bore myself outside for my conversation
with Marin and it was a slap to the ass.

"Nuclear what?" I figured I'd heard wrong.

"Waste," Marin spat through my phone. "The bill
allows secure transportation, management, and disposal
of radioactive materials within New York State and the
sovereign nations therein, via LTA if practicable."

I had read about this. Or tried to. "When is this hitting
the floor?"

"This week," she said. "Most likely Monday."

"Monday?" I said. "That's impassable. How did the bill make it this far without public comment?"

"No one wants debate," Marin explained. "When the feds started pushing for more nuclear waste interment, the state conservatives saw their chance. It's a highly probusiness bill."

"What about the other side?" I asked. "The progressives."

"We've all got nukes on the platform now. Zero carbon output. This might be the first unanimous vote in a hundred years. Making the turtle our official state reptile hit opposition."

"The skinks have a strong lobby," I said. "How come this bill is so coatroom?"

"The conservatives do not want to look like they're playing nice with the progressives. The progressives don't like to talk about nuclear waste. Everyone wants the doors closed on this one. I had to officially request a brief, through channels."

The shotgun in my head went off. The reason I knew shit about firearms was the same reason none of us knew shit about this bill. No offense means no defense. No news is good news. I'd been following the '…' story lately because that's how I've trained my news feeds. Nothing about guns.

What I had heard about energy came by way of Zeppelin, but even that was illusory. Which would seem to be a bit of stagecraft. Nothing penetrating about energy, clean or dirty. What political theater peaks through my curtains is almost exclusively from stage left. And I know lots of people who've seated themselves to see solely the right. If neither the left nor the right want to make a show of things, things don't get shown. The house goes dark.

There are not too many of us shining our lights into the unlit back stages of the world. No one has time for that. I've got to know if '…' is going to make the cut. We're all that way, our lives stuck in jobs. Tillers in the track, listening to tracks based on tracks we've heard before.

"Marin, I … Thanks," I said. "I find I have concerns."

"Understandable," Marin replied, using a pleasant tone for the first time. "This special session means someone's in a rush."

"Any idea who?"

"There's no kid stuck in a well," Marin said. "That means money is pushing the agenda. The contracts to transport nuclear waste by air will be fat."

"Enriching."

"Why the caucus?"

"Beyond my allotted time."

"Will," she blew out of a near-empty lung. "I want to say, 'call me.' I do."

"I believe you."

The phone went to white noise.

The exchange had ended better than I'd expected.

Ann poked her head out. "You are the life of this party."

"I'm recurring," I said. "Right now."

It seemed quite like a party when I slipped back in. The tone had changed. The bluster had died out, a soft breeze between gusts. Aside from the law enforcement folks, no one spoke the same dialect and yet, into their second round of drinks, they managed to communicate. The noise hushed some as I closed the porch door. Chapman continued to chat up Isla. Ann and Larry appeared bemused by what scraps of conversation they picked up. The FBI agents and Bremburg gave me their attention.

"You mentioned an arrest?" Danh asked.

"That's the objective, right?" I asked back. "Arrest Arthur Loam?"

"I can't say," Danh said. "What's your objective?"

"I can't say."

Danh smirked at Agent McClellan, then turned back to me. "You angling for a cut? Moving in on the business? Or are you all taking the easy way and going for blackmail?"

"Like I said," I said. "I can't say."

"You can't say much, for a mouthpiece."

"Irony is a hazard of my profession. What's your excuse?"

"You don't have control of this situation."

"No one does, Special Agent Danh. Not you, not me, none of us by ourselves. Look at this place ... No, my apologies. Take in this situation. I am face-to-face with friendlies because I needed a temporary task force. A posse. And not civilians thinking in sync. I required the opposite. Diverse specialties. Not a squad of cops who all think like cops, or lawyers who think like lawyers. Or merchants, or medicals or monks. Copy?"

"Oh, I copy that, Mr. Kirst," Special Agent Danh said. "It is your motivation that is in question. To be honest, I think we're helping you out. Dispersing might keep you all out of trouble."

Now I'm thinking this guy must be fifth generation law-enforcement. He didn't have it in him to see anything from more than one way, the cop way, which is always about what's lurking about. It's never *do you like this painting?* it's *do you think this painting's a forgery?*

"Do you operate a black Monte Carlo?" I asked.

Dahn's face got gnarled. "No."

"The local office has some," McClellan offered.

"The Department's had me tailed. I'm figuring the FBI pulled my file and shut out Bremburg and the Beau Fleuve PD, too, affirmative?"

Danh and McClellan looked at me with expressions they must have practiced to get that flat.

"Roger," I continued. "There are two motivations for those activities. One: you want the collar for yourselves. I don't know why you'd care, maybe the FBI has quotas, or you're targeting a promotion. Either way, I'm liking option two: you don't investigate murders — you don't care if Loam did murder Dombrowski — you are from the racketeering division. You don't want Loam, you want his organization, lock, stock, and barrels of spent uranium."

McClellan tilted her head. Her attempt at a friendly look. I have to say, it kind of worked. "Objectives aside," McClellan asked, "do you have evidence of a crime?"

"No," I answered. "But Arthur Loam might be able to help us with that."

Chapter 26

From "Tales without Interpreters"
Pastor Bowman wanted to help with the Saturday night
chicken dinner the church was putting on. He went back
to the kitchen and asked the cooks how he could pitch
in. One pointed to the bushels of fresh peaches and said,
"Those are for the cobbler. Stoning 'em would be a big
help." Pastor Bowmen didn't know much about cooking
cobbler, but he sure knew how to stone. He took the bushel
baskets out back, grabbed some rocks from the garden
and started throwing with all his earthly might.

How many interpreters does it take to change a light bulb?

Trick question. Interpreters can't change anything.

My friend Kai told me that one. He found it funny. I never did. The whole concept of being there, anywhere things happened, as an impassive presence seemed somewhat shady. That interpreters are beside events — or worse — above them. It never agreed with me. Like a bad clam. The time had come to expel it.

I stood on Bremburg's porch, inhaling the night air, and listened to my friends leave the apartment. The FBI followed. They had things to do, provided I did mine. Without throwing up.

"Call Kai." I held my silvery phone between my middle two fingers, the end with the mic between my lips. I waggled it ever so slightly, my tell, my signal to anyone who knew me well that I was bored or nervous or, in this case, a queer combination of both.

"Hazzah, Willy," Kai answered. I stopped twirling. "Feed me."

"Is Andrea with you?"

"Yes, rightly she is. You have—"

"Put her on."

"You have a question?"

"I don't want to be rude, really, put her on."

"Sure. You want her number? Can I—"

"On."

"Quite the nuciform tonight."

"Actually, I'm dehiscing. Put. Her. On."

Hushed confusion came through the speaker, swishing air and muffled voices.

"William," Andrea's voice ended the noise.

"Contact your boss. Schedule a meeting with him and myself on the platform of his Statler Zeppelin tower."

She laughed. Not a real good laugh, more of an at-you chuckle.

"Midnight tonight. Have him release the door prior to the meeting."

"Those terms are risible, Will." She tried to keep it light.

"They are also nonnegotiable. Report this: I made a site visit to the Quarantine Zone. I've developed several new prospects."

"You're going to have to up your offer."

"I'll double it," I said. "But try this. You awarded Kai the time share at Rigoletto's. Loam wanted his own interpreter on site. In case of some unforecasted event. That arrangement did not balance with you. I'm estimating that you really started to like Kai. Another unforecasted event. How's this fitting?"

"Like it needs a good tailor, William."

"I'm not sure how much you knew about your boss' plans, but I'm taking the position that you didn't want Kai at the table. So, you arranged for a substitute. Me. Now you got me and here's my deal. I like Kai, you like Kai, and Kai seems to like you. Let's keep all this status quo for now. What do you say? We'll reserve this little report for the executive level."

She took a gulp of something. I hoped, for both our sake's, it had a kick.

"I'll try to set something up."

"See you 'round the holidays."

I held my phone near my lips, puffing in and out and in and out.

"Call Sophia," I said.

The pause seemed longer than normal. A side-effect, I decided, of an elevated heart rate. The faster it beats, the slower time flows, which oddly enough, takes years off your life. I could feel them falling off my nineties, somewhere, out there in time.

"Rodger, Will," Sophia answered. "What's your status?"

"Hitting a little pocket," I said. "What's your fix?"

"I'm in the Beau, slamming and clicking," she answered. "Why? You want to get together?"

"I do," I said. "I'm going to shoot you the coordinates."

I finished up as Bremburg emerged, carrying two rocks glasses. An amber liquid lolled back and forth in each.

"What's the bullet?" he asked.

I took one of the glasses. "My sister's in."

We raised our glasses and clicked the sides.

"You got this?" he asked.

"Like shooting fish in a barrel." Which could be taken as dumb, dangerous, messy and ultimately pointless, but I don't think he saw it that way. I didn't want him to. At least one of us should be at ease.

I threw back.

Chapter 27

From "Hoe of Babylon"
'Poortage' refers to a word carried from one argot to the another, but doing a crappy-ass job of it. As in 'radical.' From the Latin 'radix', it relates to the root of things. Chemistry and Math retain the root relationship. Politics, as usual, took that meaning and twisted it. What meant reform running all the way to the core, came to refer to fringe beliefs. Hence, a radical is now someone who is far from center. A radical as poortaged to the opposite of radical. This is why we can't have nice words.

I parked in a loading zone. The car warned me and I ignored it. I opened the door to warm, dewy night air and got out into a full garbage-can stench. Rotting scraps, souring sugars, the acid air of a city that needed a hard, steady rain. Saturday nights downtown had lots of life. This corner, a little less. The Statler Hotel stood opposite a huge roundabout, with a statue in the center. It looped by City Hall, the Federal Court House, the County lock up, and some other buildings I know nothing of because none of them served drinks or hotdogs or played music. No one walked over there at night. No one else, I should say.

I rounded the corner.

The hotel was a couple hundred years old, with tall buttresses, intricate stonework, and weathered brick to prove it. It also had activity, a handful of people strolling in or out of the lobby. I went in through the main doors and sucked in a big batch of cool, sterile air. White marble pillars, black marble floor, arches and moldings and brass from about as deep in the past as American's liked to get. None of it fit me, my mood, or my mission. This place had been built to announce new sophistication — back when electric lights were the cat's pajamas and Daisy rode a bicycle built for two. It had been revived when the city scrubbed off its rust and tried again to pack its mule-tugged freight and forge foundations farther back in the basement. As if it were possible, as if a three hundred-year-old city could get past its past. Stirred or shaken, with a freshly sourced this or a twist of that, the base would always be an old spirit.

That thought made me glance in the bar as I walked by. Possibly, anyway. It could have been the hankering for another drink. It could have been that feeling you get when someone's looking at you. Because, in fact, a pair of eyes fixed on me. Black headlights worked just the same as bright ones on this jittery deer. I stopped, stunned.

Victoria sat at a high table, facing out from the bar, into the hallway. She held a martini glass between her thumb and bottom three fingers, leaving the index free to move like she was slowly shooting skeet. Victoria, my boss, beckoned.

I took a few steps back and around, to enter the bar the right way, as opposed to hoping the railing. The bar had warm lights, low chatter and enough people to keep you from feeling lonely but not enough for a crowd. The seat next to her remained open and my guess was she had maintained that status for this moment.

"William." She wore a simple white wrap that missed the shoulders. It looked cool, as in airy. "How nice. Join me."

"I have an appointment." I sat.

"You've got time." She turned a few degrees and made a slight flick of her wrist in the direction of the main bar. "They have a Pimm's Cup to die for."

"I was hoping to keep dying off my menu tonight."

"They use cucumber water for the ice."

"Sounds enchanting," I replied. "Like running into you, and you knowing my estival drink. It's like magic."

"Or diligence, patience, attention — you know, the other ways to cause an effect."

"I'm more of a wizards and witches kind of guy."

"And here I'd picked you for the gumshoe type. I thought you were wrapped up in smoke and mystery."

My drink arrived and I took a sip. Victoria had been right about the flavor. If I lived through the next thirty minutes, I'd be back for another.

"What are you doing here?" I asked.

"See," she replied. "That is exactly what I mean. William Kirst would not normally be so blunt. Not if he weren't playing detective."

"Did Loam call you himself or have a lackey pull you in?"

"Do you know why I hired you right out of school?" She eased a little curve into her neck and across her lips. She went from ice to warm bath without turning a knob. It frightened me a tad.

"My boyish charm?"

"There's that," Victoria said. "You always have that when you need it. You have everything when you need it. Interpretation is an art and a science. Those two disciplines do not mix well. They require talents in different, and sometimes competing, parts of the brain. It's a rare interpreter that masters the technical and the expressive. You are one of the rare ones."

Never in three years had she given me a complement. "Thank you," I said, trying not to appear shocked.

"You are masterful to a fault," she continued.

Ah. I shouldn't have thanked her. I should have said "no, stop," and put up my hands. Maybe we wouldn't have gotten to that second part.

"You are an immersive, William."

"Immersive. The noun form, huh?"

"You spend time with lawyers, you become argumentative. You spend time with an advertising agency, you become kinetic. With engineers you become more precise, more analytical. Do you remember the time we went to the Water Authority to facilitate negotiations? You became surly, took twenty breaks and stopped at five o'clock ... mid-sentence."

I chuckled.

"Now you are cavorting with cops. What do you think that might be doing to you?"

"I appreciate your concern." I checked my watch. "The escapade will come to an end in nineteen minutes."

"It is the next nineteen minutes that matters most. I want to make sure you are functioning with a clear and level head."

"Cops don't?"

"Cops have their goals and you have yours. Are you sure they are one in the same? When you are fully immersed it can be less than evident."

This had now been the longest conversation I had ever had with Victoria. My job interview had consisted of her walking me around a job fair, having me talk to recruiters in their professional argots. She had sized me up in situ, in a place that had both candidates and people with whom to test them. Logical, economical, smart — qualities that let her build the firm.

"I can't decide," I said. "Are you trying to impart some of your finer qualities on me — are you trying to immerse me in you to help me make an intelligent decision about the rest of my evening, or did you get a message from a wealthy client telling you one of your dogs got out. Curb him before he digs up the rhododendron."

Victoria rolled her eyes off to the right. "Why would it have to be one or the other?"

"Because I can't believe you'd let someone else jerk your chain."

Her eyes came back to me. "I let people tell me what to say all day long. That's the job. They never tell me what to do."

I stood and gulped down the rest of my cocktail. "Your plan worked. I have absorbed your confidence. Now I'm going to go upstairs and have a conversation. Not capacitate one or abet an exchange. I'm going have a talk as an active participant."

Victoria kept her eyes hard on me as she finished her drink. I couldn't tell their color in the low, honey light of the bar, but I could tell I'd knocked her off script. She'd be winging it now, which meant I might hear a tidbit of truth.

"You know recording isn't an option up there," she said.

"Ion canons keep the static down," I replied. "It seems people are willing to put up with poor communication if the alternative is a fireball the size of a city block."

"After our first year, Loam tried to renegotiate our retainer. He wanted to pay less, naturally. I said no and goodbye. He came back after a few days. He comes back every year, and every year he tries to negotiate down."

"You've known him a while, then."

"Long enough to know he's dangerous."

"Victoria," I said. "Are you worried about me?"

"I don't like losing," she returned.

"Associates or clients?"

"Like I said, why does it have to be one or the other?"

I shrugged. I had nothing more to say.

Never a good sign.

Chapter 28

From "Tales without Interpreters"
Like a lot of morbidly successful rock stars, Vlad guzzled
experiences like Moet. With a blend of charm and
intimidation, he convinced the pilot to let him take the
helm of the tour blimp. He actually showed some skill
behind the wheel, until winds off the lake changed. Vlad
sang to sooth his nerves. The pilot said, "Your pitch is off."
Vlad tuned his voice. The pilot became more insistent.
"Your pitch is too low." Vlad tightened his voice. "No,
no," The pilot lunged for the steering yoke as the blimp
lumbered into the spire of St. Margret's. "When did you
become a bloody vocal co—" Vlad didn't get to finish the
word, late as he was to join Ritchie Valens, Buddy Holly
and J.P. "The Big Bopper" Richardson.

With no airships docked or inbound, I stood alone at the top
of the tower. I walked down the short hallway to the vault-
like door that led out to the catwalk. Per my instructions to
Andrea, it whooshed opened with at the push of a button.
The door should be locked in the absence of a Zeppelin. I
picked one of Loam's towers figuring he could unlock it and
let us outside to ... get some fresh air.

The cantilevered walkway ran thirty feet into
nothingness, with all the railings and cables lawyers had
requested over the years. A good three hundred feet above
the streets, the temperature dropped a tad. A breeze couldn't
be felt down on the street brushed my skin, and hushed
the city sounds. Dots of red and white lights chased each
other through black troughs of silver haze. The buildings
of Beau Fleuve jutted up from the earth, straight fingers in

half-buried hands reaching from a grave. Reaching for me, I thought. The city wanted to pull me back down and under.

Waiting didn't bother me a bit. I planted my elbows and leaned on the railing at the far end. I could see the lake from here, lights bouncing of the ruffled black water. Lake Erie. They still spelled it with one 'e' upfront. Shunning the traditional second 'e', trying to hide something, I always figured. You could smell the lake, too. A green scent, with a hint of lively fish. It had been years since I had this kind of solitude. I obviously had no idea what to do with it, contemplating fish and seaweed and spooky waters.

I thought about playing a song. Coolio, Gangsta's Paradise,
As I walk through the valley of the shadow of death
I take a look at my life and realize there's none left....
Perfect as that song might have been for my new hardcore, thug life, I decided on no extra sounds. I'd keep all my senses on task. Besides, the wind had a soothing beat. It seemed to inhale and exhale up here. A rhythmic peace which made the breathy sound of the steel door more startling. I turned and leaned back on the metal tubing. The light from inside the tower hall almost hurt. I looked away until the doors shut.

"What's your deal?" Loam had no expression. He wore a black silk shirt, gray plaid trousers and matching jacket, buttoned. Bursting, almost. My memory had downplayed his gym-rat presence.

I motioned him forward. "Are you alone?"

"Is there a need for additional personnel?"

"You afraid of me?"

"Hardly." Loam strolled out on the platform. "You're a curiosity." Loam cocked his head and snickered, as if watching a pet who'd learned a new trick. "Why the executive session, Kirst?"

"You know why, or you wouldn't have taken this meeting after hours."

"Fair enough." He stopped a few feet from me, crossed his arms and locked his knees. "What's your position?"

"My site visit to the Zone produced several untoward results. I met people. In residence."

"And I have some interest in this?"

"They produce wine."

"Nothing comes out of the Zone."

"The brief used to read nothing out or in, but that's different as of Monday, isn't it."

Except for the crabapples he suddenly appeared to have in either cheek, Loam kept his face blank. It's probably how he'd made it so far in the competitive field of cheating and swindling. He was a difficult opponent to understand in a world where such knowing could be invaluable. He stood close enough to let me peer into his wide pores, to wallow in his cloud of spicy cologne and see the graying sprouts he'd need to shave real soon. I could see cracks of imperfection, humanity, and age. I saw a dash of weakness.

"It was my meeting with the tech writers at Novi Disposal that enhanced my understanding of your proposal," I said.

"I have nothing to do with them," Loam said. "They are my competitors."

"Exactly," I replied. "They wanted corporate intelligence. Their due diligence was poor. I knew nothing at the time. Back then. The situation has since changed for the good."

"And what do you think you know, Mr. Kirst?"

"You are going to win the contract to carry nuclear waste into the Quarantine Zone."

"I should hire you, if you can forecast that well."

"You can underbid everyone, because you are going to make money hauling in and hauling out. Wine from the Zone. Illegal, but that's just a rebottling job away."

"I see," Loam said. "Your selection of this site for our meeting has some puts and gets. The only security equipment up here is mine. There are no outside parties signing in. The anti-static capital up here screws with most other capital. So, this is truly between us and unrecorded. Because you are planning to extort a lump-sum payoff, from me, am I right? You're not whistleblowing on the vintners. That's not enough."

"Bull," I said. "We're finally on the same page."

"Bear." Loam sneered. "We are not on the same anything. You're an infinitesimal D-rated piece of human collateral I can simply round down to nothing. We can never be on the same page, because you're off the books. Good evening, Mr. Kirst."

He backed away, watching me.

"You're taking on a lot of risk here," I said fast.

Loam spread his arms, gazing at me like he'd been asked to identify my body. "No risk, no gain."

"Third parties do have knowledge of this meeting. I left contingencies plans."

"You should have planned better." He stopped at the door. To the side was a small, nearly invisible cabinet. He opened it.

I asked, "Do you want to hear my offer?"

"I shall decline at this time." He pulled out a clamp shaped like a black letter D, fixed to the end of an orange ribbon which I presumed rolled off a reel in the cabinet. He unbuttoned his jacket, revealing a nylon safety harness.

This wasn't going the way I intended. "You can't dismiss me."

"That is where you are wrong." He clicked the clamp to his harness. He would not be falling to his death tonight.

"If I don't make a specific call at a specific...." I let that thought trail off. I couldn't sell that particular lie to such a seasoned and successful liar. I had to jump to a different track. "Don't you understand? I put you in the red, chief. I figured out your plan to lease the Zeppelin tower, before word of the nuclear waste permit went public. Me. I figured it out ... I own you."

He moved towards me, trying to snicker, but his upper lip curled too much, pulling back tarp on a moist, pink stall of champing whitish teeth. "You own nothing, mouthpiece. Not even your own life."

"Do not threaten me." I took a step towards him.

"You so thoroughly called at the wrong time," Loam said. "I honestly cannot believe you followed me this far as you're too incompetent to recognize your position."

"Incompetent? You mismanaged this whole project and now you're going to pay for it. 'Burial,' you said. That's what attracted me. Not *interment*, but *burial* as in *grounds*. Your undue regard for exposure to Native American concerns put up a red flag. A tribal dispute was one of the few details that might have stopped you. Were you always stupid or has your intelligence depreciated with advancing age?"

"You ignorant little call." Loam removed a small, black box from his breast pocket. At first I thought it was his phone. Then I saw the prongs. A zapper. One touch and I'd be unconscious. Loam approached, carefully, arms wide, as if trying to corner a mouse in his garage.

I had made a mistake. I just didn't know what mistake I'd made.

"You're going zap me?" I glanced up, over his head. "And then what, toss me over?"

"You are a troubled young man," Loam said. "Suicidal, your friend Kai will support."

"I reported my contingency plans."

"I am so advised."

Even if I managed to grab him, the harness would keep him from joining me on the pavement. And I still didn't have what I needed. I still didn't understand my mistake.

Loam lunged at me. I dodged to the right, barely, stunned that he'd try to stun me. A middle aged, rich guy doing his own dirty work?

"Don't you have people for this?" I backed down the catwalk, in the direction of the end.

"If you want a job done right—" He lunged again, stabbing the zapper at me. I jumped back, peddling, shuffling, wishing real hard I wouldn't run out of catwalk any time soon, then I hit the peak of the railing with my tailbone. End of the little road.

His face had tightened. I'd fomented his anger. Made him shut up and get to work, the antithesis of what I needed.

Because I did it wrong. As Victoria thought I would, as I always do, as I was, am, and forever shall be. Wrong.

Loam snapped his buzzer hand like a cobra. I caught his wrist three inches from my face. His other hand caught my other hand. I had at least twenty-five years less muscle degradation on him. He had fifty pounds on me, better footing and, as my back started to bend the wrong way, leverage. And he didn't need much advantage. One touch of those metal fangs. One touch—

Was the antithesis of what I needed.

What I needed was the antithesis. What's the opposite of immersive? What was the flip side of Loam?

"I did this all wrong," I said. I let *me* out — ashamed, disappointed, and most of all, honest.

"Yes. You. Did." Loam bent me back even more, inching the stunned towards my left ear.

"What?" I used my most earnest voice. "What did I do wrong?"

"You didn't learn from Dombrowski," Loam said. "He thought he could make a deal, too." Loam pushed harder. "He had timing and location. I had a step ahead. Sound familiar?"

"Sounds lacking." I pushed back. "Try two steps ahead. That's where you really want to be."

He threw his body into it. My arms cried. My fingers slipped around his wrist. Then he pulled back just a tad.

"Cease and desist," I huffed. "It's over."

"For you, yes." He'd realized something. He could crash my hands together. One touch—

Flood lights blasted us.

"Drop, lower, release your weapon," came from overhead. Loam cantered back, eyebrows crushed together. He looked up, shielding his eyes. A Zeppelin's propellers spun up to a roar. They brought the great, gray beast lower and closer. Bremburg leaned out of the gondola, hand to the side of his mouth. "Drop, lower, release your weapon now."

"He means unload that zapper before you take on an unrecoverable loss."

Loam looked at me, his face calm as ever. His eyelids sank and rose slowly, like he might fall asleep. He let the zapper fall to the floor. He did not move as the airship swung around, hooked the guy-post with its nose, and descended farther, the pewter-white girth blocking out the stars.

"I hereby cancel my contract to provide you with interpreter services," I told Loam.

"I was going to fire you anyway," he replied. "For cause. You'll lose your license."

"You've lost everything."

A set of six metallic clunks told us the gondola and platform had come together. I stepped forward as the railing gave way. People ran. Bremburg and another uniformed cop flew by, physically arresting Loam.

"William," came from behind me. "What's your status?"

I turned just in time to keep my sister from knocking me over. She hugged me so hard I thought my neck might burst.

"Thanks for the hop," I said. "Was it much trouble?"

"Playful." She stepped back. "Some cross winds off the lake ... Running silent is the devil, still...."

Agent Danh walked by, nodding once. Agent McClellan stopped next to us.

"Everything all right, Mr. Kirst?"

"Ten-twenty-four" I replied.

"We heard everything. Thanks. To both of you." She started to move on, keeping her gaze on me for an extra beat. On me. A look. Over her shoulder.

"My sister," I said. "This is my—"

Sophia stopped me. "She's not your type."

Chapter 29

From "Tales without Interpreters"
The Director of New Projects came down to the conference
room to meet with the captain. "The project is by the
board," he said with a grin. A grin? Really? That infuriated
the captain more than anything. This man told him he
loved his idea. The Board would certainly want to fund
whale watching from a real two-masted schooner. The
captain jumped up. "You tell them I'm taking my proposal
to your competitors." He stormed out, leaving the Director
of New Projects three sheets to the wind.

Victoria looked like a magic marker gliding down the hallway, her navy suit so tight around her one-dimensional body. She put one foot directly in front of the other, drawing a thin, unseen line on the shiny, speckled floor. I sat on one of two cushy benches designated for praying, cursing, replaying the recent past, and waiting on fate. The situation grew crueler the longer I sat there, out in the open, on a crossroads, on full display so that others could think to themselves, *I wonder what he did? Is he on the verge of hugging the next person who pushes through those oak double doors or folding into a wet puddle of despair and remorse? And should I watch? Should I walk more slowly and try to glimpse the drama?*

The doors had opened much sooner than I'd expected. Victoria had been in for twenty-one minutes. A quick decision is generally great or terrible, depending on whom you speak with prior to your hearing. Nobody really knows what they're talking about half the time. Weather, politics, the Yankee's chances, your future — if people stuck to what they knew the world would be a much quieter place.

"You're clear," Victoria said as she passed me. I can only assume she was speaking to me, rather than someone down the hall, as there was no one else around.

"Thank God." I tipped my head back and closed my eyes.

"Pretty much."

"What did they say?"

"I just told you." She continued down the corridor. I had to hop up and follow.

"I didn't violate my oath? No extraneous divulgence?"

"It's pass/fail. Taking video and audio from beyond the ion bubble was smart, but you receive no pats on the head for being clever, no claxons for skirting too close to the edge. The board reviewed the video of your exchange with Loam and agreed you never uttered any privileged information. Your license remains in force."

"And you?" I asked, catching up. "The firm ... I'm sorry you had to defend my honor."

"It is my job. You did yours, so I damn well better do mine, don't you think?"

"I ... ah ... makes this—"

"See you back at the office."

"Not really."

She stopped.

"I mean, you will, for two weeks."

Victoria glanced at me without moving her head.

"You are giving me notice now? After successfully defending your livelihood?"

"It wouldn't have done me much good to resign before, would it."

Her eyes were gray, I realized for the first time, as she stared at me. Pointy at the ends, up turned, like two swords on the wall of a club to which I'd never be sponsored.

"Fine, then," she said.

"I'm going to freelance."

"Yes."

"The firm ... it keeps you in a tract."

"I stopped caring seven seconds ago." She walked on — snap, snap, snapping down the hall.

I walked out through the big front doors and down the steps. It smelled, again, like it might rain. Yet another reason to smile. At the bottom of the steps, across the sidewalk, a car sat right between two 'No Parking' signs. The serious signs, with just a picture of a wheeled vehicle encircled and slashed. No room for interpretation there. It took me a second, then I recognized the vehicle. An unmarked police cruiser.

"Hey," came from my right. Bremburg leaned against the building.

"Nice to see you, Detective."

He approached, carrying a parcel in his hand, the size of a personal pizza box, wrapped in brown paper. "What's the verdict?"

"I can speak freely," I replied. "How's your investigation going?"

"Loam lawyered up. We're looking for those Novi Disposal Logistics staff writers now. Thanks for the tip on that playground you hit. Mondo's? Some of those kids had barrel cameras on their weapons. Got lots of clean footage of the skells putting a pistol to you."

"And me? Peeing myself?"

"You did fine. We let Olivia Carl's dad go. So, an innocent guy didn't get sent up for this. You should feel good about that." Bremburg handed me the package. "Congratulations."

"Thanks," I said. "But it really isn't required."

"Open it."

I tore away the brown paper, revealing a frayed and faded paperback book.

"It got left with me years ago by an ex I ain't never going to partner with again. Thought it might serve you better than my closet floor."

I turned the book over. *Bob Dylan: The Complete Lyrics*.

"Thank you very much," I said.

"So," Bremburg started. "You hear about the homicide last night in Delaware Park?"

"Negative," I said, willing my eyes to say, *go on.*

If you enjoyed this read...

Please leave a review.

It takes less than five minutes, and it really does make a difference.

Reviews should answer at least three basic questions.
(But won't give the story away.):

- Did you like the book? *("Loved the book! Can't wait for the Next!")*
- What was your favorite part? *(Characters, plot, location, scenes.)*
- Would you recommend the book?

Your review will help other readers discover this book. Consider leaving your review on Amazon, Barnes and Noble, Apple iBooks, KOBO, Goodreads, BookBub, Facebook, Instagram and/or your own website.

Brian Hades, publisher

To leave a review on Amazon

~ Even if the book was not purchased on Amazon ~

1. Go to amazon.com. Sign into your Amazon account. If you do not have an Amazon account, you need to create one and activate it by making a purchase. Amazon will check to see that your account is active before allowing you to leave a review. Amazon has some restrictions, such as not leaving a bias review. For more information on Amazon's policies please read Amazon's Community Guidelines for book reviews:

   https://www.amazon.com/gp/help/customer/display.html?nodeId=GLHXEX85MENUE4XF

2. Search for and find The Tongue Trade by Michael J. Martineck, then click on the book's details page.

3. Scroll down to find the Write a Customer R Write a customer review eview button. Click it.

4. Select your star rating. A rating of 5 is best, 1 is worst.

5. If you have a photo or video to share, add it to the upload box.

6. Add a headline.

7. Write your review.

8. Press the SUBMIT button

To leave a review on Barnes and Noble
~ Even if the book was not purchased on BN.com ~

1. Go to barnesandnoble.com and sign up for an account.
2. Search for and find The Tongue Trade by Michael J. Martineck, then click on the book's details page.
3. Scroll down to the review section and click on the Write a Review button.
4. Select your star rating. A rating of 5 is best, 1 is worst.
5. Add a review title.
6. Write your review.
7. Add a photo if you wish.
8. Select if you would recommend this book to a friend.
9. Select appropriate TAGs.
10. Indicate if your review contains spoilers.
11. Select the type of reader that best describes you (optional).
12. Enter your location (optional).
13. Enter your email address.
14. Checkmark that you agree to the terms and conditions.
15. Press the POST REVIEW button.

About the Author

Michael J. Martineck started writing stories when he was twelve. Over the years he's written short stories, comic book scripts, articles, and a quintet of novels.

DC Comics published a couple of Martineck's stories in the early '90s. Planetmag, Aphelion and a couple of other long-dead e-zines helped out in '00s.

His early long works include The Misspellers, and The Wrong Channel.

EDGE Science Fiction and Fantasy published Cinco de Mayo, his first novel for adults, and finalist for the Alberta Reader's choice Award. Followed by The Milkman (which won an IPPY for best science fiction novel, and an Eric Hoffer finalist) and its sequel, The Link Boy.

Our Little Secret Press recently published Untouchable, a cocktail of romance and crime with a dash of weird.

He currently teaches English at two local colleges, and lives and writes in Grand Island, New York with his beautiful wife and two children.

Need something new to read?
If you liked The Tongue Trade, you should also
consider these other EDGE titles.

——< >——

Cinco de Mayo

by Michael J. Martineck

Secrets: some feel freed having them out. Others will kill to keep them.

On May 5, in a flash of pain, every man, woman and child on the planet receives a second set of memories. A new name, a new language, a whole new life slips into their minds, along side their own.

In Chicago, a transit worker knows enough about the Aryan Brotherhood to mark him for death.

In Abu Dhabi, a playboy experiences modern day slavery.

In New York an advertising executive shares the memories of a blind railroad worker in China.

In this transparent world of instant intimacy, no one is left untouched... Everyone has secrets!

For more on Cinco de Mayo visit:

tinyurl.com/edge2038

——<>——

The Milkman
A Free World Novel

by Michael J. Martineck

In the near future, corporation rules every possible freedom. Without government, there can be no crime. And every act is measured against competing interests, hidden loyalties and the ever-upward pressure of the corporate ladder.

Any quest for transparency is as punishable as an act of murder. But one man has managed to slip the system, a future-day Robin Hood who tests dairy milk outside of corporate control and posts the results to the world.

When the Milkman is framed for a young girl's murder and anonymous funding comes through for a documentary filmmaker in search of true art beneath corporate propaganda, eyes begin to turn and soon the hunt is on.

Can the man who created the symbol of the Milkman, the only one who knows what really happened that bloody night, escape the corporate rat maze closing around him? Or is it already too late?

For more on The Milkman visit:

tinyurl.com/edge2075

————<>————

The Link Boy
A Free World Novel

by Michael J. Martineck

Our post-government future has no laws, but plenty of right and wrong.

An assassin, a priest and a schoolteacher walk into a secret nuclear power plant – to Edwin McCallum, detective by trade and artist by desire – there's something wrong with this picture. He's going to figure out what it is if it kills him.

The Link Boy is the second novel set in the Free World, a post-government future, where there are no laws. Just bottom lines.

For more on The Link Boy visit:

tinyurl.com/edge2025

For more EDGE titles and information about upcoming speculative fiction please visit us at:

www.edgewebsite.com

Don't forget to sign-up for our Special Offers

Made in the USA
Middletown, DE
10 September 2024

60049916R00135